HIS TREAT

PENELOPE BLOOM

1

EMILY

Droplets of water snailed their way down the passenger window of Lilith's car. She was pretty much my only real friend, and she was also my only access to private transportation around the city. I was admittedly over-bundled against the light chill of the early Fall morning, but I'd been waiting all summer to wear my comfy clothes, and I could always peel some layers off if I got hot.

I ran my fingertips over the letter in my jacket pocket. I'd made such a habit of carrying it around and re-reading it that I'd ended up turning the paper soft, but I still brimmed with equal parts excitement and dread when I touched it. The letter meant a new start. A chance to take a real step toward my dream. For years, it felt like I'd been circling the idea of becoming a real, professional artist with about the same drunken lack of direction as a toddler on a bike with one training wheel. I never could just go in a straight line, and every time I thought I was getting closer, I'd zip right past it and have to circle around to start the process all over again.

This time was going to be different. The letter in my jacket *was* that straight line. It was a direct flight, and even I couldn't mess this one up. I just had to show up at the airport in January. It would be as simple as breathing. Then again, I had sleep apnea, and apparently breathing wasn't always the simplest thing in the world for me, so that was a bad analogy. The point was, I could do this.

It was my favorite time of year. It was Fall. Summer was over, or at least coughing up its final, dying words. I knew summer was supposed to be the best. It was the time of swimsuits, parties, picnics, and throwing a frisbee to your golden retriever in the park. *Yeaah! Go, Summer!* Except that had never been my reality. For me, Summer was underboob sweat, staying in all day because I'd rather not melt outside, and getting the yearly sunburn that reminds me why I don't ever want to get a sunburn again. Oh, and the influx of air conditioner commercials about "beating the heat" that pop up on the radio.

Well, screw you very much, Summer. It was over for another year, and now it was the time of horror movie marathons and for M&Ms to put out their Halloween themed commercials. The leaves were turning every shade of yellow, orange, and red you could imagine. Rainy morning or not, I couldn't help feel the familiar excitement of the coming holidays. This morning had been the day I waited for all year—the one where you can *feel* the change as soon as you step outside. The air had that crisp, energizing quality that made me want to tackle my day, even if tackling my day should've had the appeal of tackling a three-hundred pound, sweaty man with patchy body hair.

I'd always loved Halloween. Maybe not so much for the holiday itself, but more because it was the first wave of the cold-weather holidays I spent all year looking forward to. Except for this year, they'd be more than just another round of holidays. They'd be the last few months before I flew overseas and started art school in Paris. No matter how many times I thought about it or how often I re-read the acceptance letter, it still didn't seem real.

"Stop looking so happy over there," Lilith groaned. She wore a thick bar of eye-liner, a perfectly straight row of black bangs, and a black lace choker on her pale, slender neck. She had the perfect porcelain skin and features of a beauty queen, but she wore a constant expression that let you know, without any shadow of a doubt, she resented the fact that she had to exist.

If she had to be here, she'd make sure the universe knew it had made a mistake.

I'd had the good fortune of meeting her in high school, and we'd been unlikely friends ever since. Maybe it was because she only survived school from my notes and study help, or maybe it was that I'd managed to save her from the worst of the bullies she seemed to attract. Either way, I liked her, and I guess it was for the same reason people inexplicably liked cats. Want to poop on my pillow because I went out of town for a day? Want to pee directly outside your litter pan even though it's perfectly clean? Or maybe you want to just make sure gravity still works for the tenth time this week and knock my drink to the floor. That was Lilith, well, minus the bathroom habits, as far as I knew. Deep down. *Deep, deep,* down, I knew she still needed affection just like everyone else. And I liked how hard she tried to pretend she didn't.

"I said stop it," she repeated in her usual deadpan. "I can see you smiling from the corner of my eyes. It's going to make me barf."

"Can't help it. It's *Fall*," I said the words in a singsong voice, partly because I knew outward happiness was like Lilith's kryptonite.

She grimaced. "Good, then maybe those disgusting creatures you're trying to grow in our kitchen will die soon."

"Plants, Lilith. They're called plants, and considering they're inside, I'm sorry to say they will probably survive."

"Accidents happen, though." She didn't take her eyes from the road, but I thought I saw a little glimmer of pleasure in them as her thoughts turned murderous.

"What kind of person doesn't like plants?"

"They smell."

"Ooh!" I said, pointing to a billboard on the side of the highway. "Pumpkin Spiced Lattes! We're half-way through October, and I haven't even had one yet. We have to. *Please*."

"Ugh." She gave me a sideways look—showing no concern for the fast-moving traffic in front of us as she stared me down

A nervous smile twitched across my face. "The road," I said quietly.

She languidly dragged her eyes back to the road. "It's not going anywhere."

"Technically, no, it's not. But *we are*. At about... Ninety," I said, leaning to the side to glance at the speedometer. I laughed, but my heart was pounding. I was pretty sure a few more seconds would've had us careening off the road to our fiery deaths. I had too much to live for to die young. The last season of Game of Thrones was still coming, I had never eaten a poached egg, and my bucket list still had at least ten items left unchecked, starting with ice skating with a gorgeous guy at night to the soundtrack of *Dirty Dancing*.

In all seriousness, if I died before I made it to art school in Paris... I was definitely going to come back to haunt Lilith. I'd use my artistic skills to draw ghostly penises in the fogged up glass of her shower doors, and they wouldn't be the high-school variety of graffiti penis. They'd be disturbingly detailed and lifelike. I'd... well, actually, that was about as far as my haunting creativity went. But if the time came, I'd think of something better.

Lilith shrugged at being reminded to watch the road. It was hard to say when she was amused, but I thought I could sense it radiating off her like heat. I probably seemed innocent to the world and breakable to her, even after the years we'd known each other. In her cat-like way, I think she was pawing me closer to the edge of a long, hard drop to the floor just to see what would happen.

I looked out the window as we took the exit. Stores had already started stocking the shelves with Halloween gear from candy corn to pumpkins, and I'd watched no less than two horror movie marathons, even though I had the same tolerance for being startled as a chihuahua on the Fourth of July. Freddy Krueger scared me the most. I mean, what's scarier than a guy who gets you in your dreams? At least with the other bad guys, you can *not* be the horror movie bimbo who doesn't realize that basements equal death, upstairs equals death, and barns full of thrashing equipment *definitely* equal death. Honestly, if I was in a horror movie, I'd gather up all my friends, look in the mirror, and try to figure out which one of us looked most like the cute girl next door. Everybody else was dead, and the guy who looked most like a jock was probably secretly the killer. Predictable or not, I still watched horror movies from behind a big pillow.

I told Lilith she could park and let me run in to grab the coffees, partly because I wanted a taste of the weather, but more because I'd seen how much she frightened fast-food workers. She once told me how she had found a dead fly, saved it in a zip-lock bag, and then dropped it in her fries to get free food at a restaurant. The worst part was I was pretty sure she didn't really care about saving the money. I think she just liked tormenting people.

I wrapped my scarf a little tighter around my neck. Yes, *my scarf*. It was scarf weather, and I don't know if I loved anything more than wrapping what was basically a baby sized blanket around my neck and nuzzling into it all day. It made me wish we could bring back capes. I'd never seen it in one of those medieval shows or movies, but I'd bet my life that people spun their capes around and used them as blankets when they were just hanging out around the castle.

Just feeling the crisp air outside made me want to skip and

clap my hands together, but I knew Lilith would probably sponta-
neously combust if she caught that much happiness in the
rearview mirror, so I controlled myself.

I managed to get our coffees without traumatizing anyone
and slid back into the car a few minutes later. Lilith took the
coffee from me and sipped it. She groaned. "Ugh. Disgusting."

"What?" I asked. "Did they mess it up?"

"No. It's fine. I knew it would taste like this."

I raised an eyebrow, waiting for her to explain.

She glared at me. "It's easier to hate everyone who drinks
these if I remember how gross they are."

"Riiight," I said, nodding like I understood. I sipped my drink
and then paused. I expected her to laugh, maybe even just a little,
but her face showed no expression.

I smiled to myself. She might not think she was funny, but I
enjoyed Lilith and her... *moments*. She definitely had the same
kind of charm of a cat. They might act like they hated you and
were too good for you, but you just knew they still wanted
scratches even if they'd never actually admit it. I wondered what
Lilith would do if I scratched behind her ears, but decided she
could do more damage to me than a cat, so I kept my hands to
myself. I still planned to find a way to make her smile eventually,
even if it meant I'd have to bring her a dead bird.

We pulled up to the retirement home a little while later.

"Want me to walk you in?" asked Lilith.

I grinned. "No thanks, mom."

"Whatever. I'm gassy anyway. Probably better if I don't move
around too much right now."

"Believe it or not, I could've gone all day without knowing
that."

"It's your lucky day. I'm running a two for one special."

"What? On things I didn't need to know?"

She nodded.

I could see she was waiting for permission and had a feeling I was going to regret it, but I sighed. "Okay. Go ahead."

"I see a gray man with no face who stands in the corner of my room some nights. He watches me sleep. I wake up paralyzed, and I can't move anything but my eyes—"

"Perfect!" I interrupted because I already felt chills rolling across my skin. "That should help the insomnia I've been dealing with. I'm going to go teach some grumpy seniors to paint now. Thanks for the ride."

"Oh. William is going to be there today. It's on his schedule. Just a head's up."

William Chamberson was Lilith's boss. She worked as his secretary, and I wasn't sure if she was giving me a head's up because she thought I still had a crush on the man, but I'd never had one to begin with, whether she believed me or not. My middle school boyfriend cheated on me by holding hands with another girl just a few days after we'd officially announced we were "going out." So, yeah, I was basically an expert in the kind of life-changing pain unfaithfulness can cause. William was married, and my inner middle schooler would, *like*, never even think about having a crush on a married man, even if he was drop-dead gorgeous and charming.

William was a twin. His brother was Bruce Chamberson, and they were the CEOs of a multi-million dollar corporation. I'd met both of them a couple times in the few weeks I'd been running painting classes here. One of the seniors was William's grand-mother-in-law, and his wife, brother, and brother's wife regularly came by for poker night with the seniors.

Bruce was the buttoned-up Superman type, with a jawline that could break through brick walls faster than the Kool-Aid man in a 90s commercial, eyes that could make you break a sweat, and the lean, muscular body to match. His hair was always perfectly in place, and it only took a few seconds of watching him to see that he either had O.C.D. or was dangerously close. If you liked your men... well, actually, if you liked *men* in general, then it would've been hard to find fault with him. Except the whole being married part, of course.

Then there was William. If Bruce was Superman, William was what Superman would look like if he liked to party, had never met a comb, and had a slight problem with kleptomania. Together, they were an unlikely pair, but it was highly entertaining to watch them clash, which they always seemed to do.

When I first learned Lilith was working as a secretary for some ultra-powerful businessman, I'll admit, I wondered what kind of boss could put up with her. As soon as I met William, I got it. Lilith was the scheming cat, and William was... I guess he was more like a fox with a little bit of a puppy's enthusiasm and good-naturedness thrown in. He seemed carefree and innocent at times, but there was a cunning genius hiding behind his easygoing nature. I could imagine the amusement in his eyes if Lilith dropped her deadpan humor on an important client or give someone the cold shoulder because she was in the middle of a text.

I carried a small bag of supplies in through the front door, greeted the familiar faces on my way in, and started setting up in the recreational room they'd given me as a classroom. The money from this gig wasn't great, but it was money, and it was a job related to art. That was a win, in my book. Ever since I'd set my sights on being an artist, I'd carried a chip on my shoulder. Nobody ever thought twice about making jokes when they learned what I wanted to do. "Oh, you're an artist? So which Starbucks do you work at?"

They could all stuff it. Because I didn't work at a Starbucks. I worked at... Well, I worked at a retirement home, and sometimes picked up odd jobs. Besides, when I *had* worked at a coffee place, it wasn't a Starbucks, thank you very much. It was actually a Starbucks copycat, which might have been worse. Still, they could stuff it.

I was setting up what each student would need at their table when I heard a voice I didn't recognize outside. I craned my neck to look into the hall and saw the man who was speaking. One of my eyebrows arched involuntarily.

I liked what I saw, and so did my eyebrows—one of them, at least. I had the oddest hint of familiarity about him. He looked kind of like a guy I knew from high school, but I'd gone to high school in a middle-of-nowhere town outside the city, so the coincidence was bordering on impossible.

He was straight-backed and built like an athlete. His hair was cut short and dark, and my eyes immediately sank to his mesmerizing lips. He was clearly very passionate about whatever he was saying, but I paid about as much attention to his words as a high schooler at the end of seventh period.

He was *that* guy. The guy you dream up when the lights are dimmed, and you're five minutes into a bubble bath. When candles are flickering beside the tub, and you've got a little silky smooth music floating through the air.

I could've authored a few thousand fantasy situations right then and there. *Fifty Shades of That Guy.* One where I'm standing beside my broken down car on the side of the road—forget the fact that I don't own a car—and he plants his tattooed hands on the hood and takes a look. "*I'm going to need to get under your hood, miss. And it's going to be a dirty job. And I'll have to use my biggest tool. My penis. I'm going to have sex with you.*" Yeah, my dream guys aren't very subtle.

Or maybe I'd be cornered by three hooded men in a dark alley and he'd come in swinging. Once the bad guys were on the floor, he'd scoop me into those chiseled arms and whisper sweet nothings into my ear the whole way back to his apartment.

"*I lost my dentures.*"

It took me an unnerving moment to realize the words hadn't

come from Mr. Fantasy's lips, but from the infamous Grammy, who had walked up beside me. She was William's grandmother-in-law, and she was the quintessential misbehaved class clown of the retirement home.

"O-okay..." I said.

"And I found Earl's," she said, bursting out in laughter as she smiled and flashed a pair of horribly fitting teeth.

I gagged a little. "Why would you—what?"

"The bastard beat me in poker last night. Now he's going to be beating his food into a liquid if he plans to eat." She cackled again as she hobbled toward her seat. She moved like she was a frail old woman, but I'd seen through her act. She could move with the ease of someone much younger, but she liked to play the part of the sweet old granny because it helped her get away with more of her shenanigans.

I tried to shake the image of Earl's teeth in her mouth and refocus on the wonderful moment I was having.

The man was talking to William Chamberson, who noticed me and started heading my way. Now both men were coming toward me, and in a moment of panic, I almost ran.

I calmed down—barely—and faked a smile that hopefully showed I wasn't about to need a change of pants.

"Ryan," William said, gesturing to me. "This is Emily. Emily, this is Ryan. He took over running my wife's bakeries when the TV side of her business took off. And it so happens he's in need of an artist."

Ryan. Even the name was familiar. I must have done some serious memory repression in my high school days because I was having trouble putting a name to the face of my cupcake baking tormentor from all those years ago. I could've sworn it was Ryan, though. Up close, the feeling of familiarity had only grown stronger, too.

Ryan reached to shake my hand. *So formal.* I swallowed and

reached to grab his hand, even though in all my fantasy scenarios, our first contact would be a kiss.

I completely missed the lock-in procedure and ended up squeezing his middle and index fingers instead of his whole hand. Somehow, he managed to smoothly cover my mistake by pulling my hand gently toward him in an old-fashioned kind of maneuver that had me blushing.

"Hi," I said.

He narrowed his eyes and looked at me. If I didn't know better, I'd say he was feeling the same sense of déjà vu. His head tilted a little, and it looked like he might say something, but he gave an almost imperceptible shake of his head.

"So you're the artist? William has talked up your work a lot. I'm excited to see it."

"I mean, I'm poor, and I like to draw pictures. I also wrestle with a lot of insecurities, self-doubt, and emotional pain. I think that qualifies me as an artist, right?"

He grinned and turned his head to William. "I'll take her."

"Where?" I asked.

Both men held back laughter.

Where? Did I seriously just say that? I felt like I needed one of those old-fashioned fans to cool off, or maybe just a big burlap sack to put over my head.

"Figuratively speaking," Ryan said. "Sorry. I'm getting ahead of myself. I'm putting on a Halloween party for everyone at The Bubbly Baker and Galleon. It's kind of a team-building thing. At least that's my excuse for using William's money."

The Bubbly Baker. My memory filled with images of the guy I'd known in high school and how we'd been paired together in Home Ec class our first day of senior year. He was the typical, popular jock, and he was dating the most obnoxiously gorgeous and mean girl in the school. I'd expected him to slack off and want me to do all the work, but he had really seemed to love cooking, and he had been good at it. It was the same guy. It had to be.

As soon the thought crossed my mind, it all came back in a rush. The way he hadn't stood up for me when his girlfriend, Haisley, had embarrassed me in front of half the school, or how he'd let her make up a story about me and never defended me. To top it all off, he'd even taken credit for smearing a cupcake *we baked together* across my senior art project.

The only thing stopping me from stomping on his foot and giving him a few choice words was that I felt fairly certain he'd never actually been the one to do it. His girlfriend had been sneering victoriously at me the whole time, and the Ryan I had known seemed much more like the kind of guy to take the fall for someone than to do something like that.

So I never knew the truth, but none of it felt quite so life-shatteringly bad now, especially after so many years had passed. We were kids, and we did stupid things. Yes, I'd hated him, but right now, he was an opportunity for a job. Besides, it had been years and years, so it would be ridiculous for me to still hold a grudge, right?

"Ass." William was looking at his phone and didn't seem to actually care about Ryan's admission. "Hey, it looks like I'm about to get into a bidding war on eBay. Gotta leave you two astute business-people to the contract negotiations."

"eBay? People still use that?" Ryan asked.

"Uh, yes. I buy shit on eBay all the time."

"Like what?"

A mischievous glint entered William's eyes. He waggled his eyebrows mysteriously and backed away. "All kinds of things," he said, then turned and left.

Ryan shook his head. "Probably dildos."

"Definitely dildos," I agreed. My stomach was practically bursting with nervous butterflies, but there was a friendliness in Ryan's eyes that was at odds with his rugged looks. I'd never dream of talking about dildos with a guy I'd just met again for the first time since high school, especially not one I'd sworn was a mortal enemy, even in my bodice-ripping fantasy world.

I thought about asking him if he remembered me, but what if he'd rescind the job offer if he did?

"So do you have any samples of your work? A portfolio, or anything?"

His words hung in the air. I felt time slow down, like the potential of the moment had a crushing gravity of its own. Behind the innocent words, I felt his curiosity—his interest. I felt it crackling through the air like electricity, and all I needed to do was reach out and grab it. In some ways, making things right with him felt like it'd cover up an old, long-forgotten scar. In other ways, I thought it might rip it back open.

"You could sit in on my class," I said. My head spun a little when I heard my own words, just as innocent as his but carrying their own hidden meaning. I didn't tell him I'd email him my portfolio or even offer to show him several of the sketches I had just a few steps away in my art bag. I couldn't help it. On any other day, I might've had the willpower to let the moment slide harmlessly by, but today? Today I felt the unshakable excitement of changing seasons and the coming holidays. It felt like a day for taking chances and doing reckless things, and I couldn't stop myself. "We're doing the classic Van Gogh recreation of Starry Night, but in Halloween colors. It's kind of an art cliché by now, but they've all been asking when we're going to do Starry night, so..."

"Didn't Van Gogh cut his penis off or something and mail it to his girlfriend?"

I grinned. "His ear. I can't remember if he mailed it or delivered it by hand, though. I guess you'd want something like that to get there fresh, right?"

"Well, then you forgot the most important detail. That's like the difference between a break-up text and doing it in person."

"Right, because ear or penis, what's the difference? But the delivery method..."

He nodded. "I've seen paintings of the guy. He probably had a lot more use for his ear than his penis."

I covered a smile with my hand and shook my head at him. "If you think some jokes about famous artists are going to make me like you, you're right." I was scared at how quickly I could feel it happening. The same easy conversation that had flowed between us back then came now like no time had passed at all. I remembered how quickly I'd fallen for him, and how much it had stung when he returned my teenaged girl crush with coldness.

"Who says I want you to like me? I'm just here for the practice. My dream is to become famous enough that when I cut off a body part, they'll make high school kids learn about it for centuries."

I gave him a wry look. "I'll make you a deal. Sit through my class, and then I'll tell you how much your self-mutilation would rock the art world when I've seen what you can do."

"Perfect. You do have supplies for finger-painting, right?"

I rolled my eyes, but smiled once I'd turned my back to him and got back to setting up the room. My heart was pounding from our quick conversation, and I felt giddier than I had in a long time, especially from talking to a guy. He was shockingly handsome and had the kind of quick, playful personality I liked.

I didn't even know if he was single, or what his intentions were beyond his supposed need for an artist. *God*, for all I knew, he could still be with Haisley. I made a quick promise to myself. If he was, first, I'd find a way to ruin her day, and second, I'd run as far from him as I possibly could. There were limits to my capacity for forgiveness.

What I *did* know was he had a way of making me feel like I was straight back in high school, where something as simple as a glance could set my heart pounding and make my skin burn. He'd given me more than a glance though, *hadn't he?*

I took a deep, calming breath. All I had to do was remind myself about art school. No matter who Ryan had become or what he wanted, that was priority number one. Paris. My future. My dreams. Everything depended on me stepping on an airplane in January and setting off for the new chapter in my life. Hopefully it'd be the part of the book where things got interesting. So far, the book of my life had been the parts you skim while you decide if it's worth forking over a few bucks.

I just needed to remember. I had a life to think about, and the last thing I needed was to fall for some guy who would make me think I had a reason to stay and miss my chance.

But I *did* need a real job. As much as I loved art night at the retirement home, it wasn't exactly the Sistine Chapel.

I started my lesson and stammered my way through the brief reminder on mixing paints and how to set up a color palette for a larger project.

I stumbled over my words more than once because I couldn't stop stealing glances at him. Ryan wasn't just good-looking. It was like he'd been carved out of a chunk of crystallized female desire and plopped right in front of me. He was exactly my recipe of sexy. Confident, but not in the in-your-face kind of way. Dark, heavy eyebrows, dark hair, and a look somewhere between action hero and the male lead in a romance movie. I could imagine him punching Russians at the helm of a hijacked boat or picking up girls in a rainstorm while he professed his undying love—okay, who am I kidding, I was picturing him picking me up in said rainstorm.

It had either been way, *way* too long since I had any serious attention from a guy, or Ryan was something special.

I could almost feel my brain mentally flicking me for attention, like it was trying to say, *you know what else is special, ovaries for brains? Paris! Art school. Your professional and financial future. Your dreams.*

My ovaries were too busy running through ridiculous fantasy

after ridiculous fantasy to hear. As long as I was looking right at Mr. Dreamboat, there was going to be no logic bouncing around in my skull. It was all hearts and little kissy-face emojis. Even reminding myself what a jerk he'd been in the end back in high school didn't help. That was, what, one million years ago? Two? How could I fault him and those intense, smoldering light-brown eyes for something that happened so long ago?

Ryan seemed to actually be very focused on doing a good job, but he was adorably bad at it. I was relieved to see he was kidding about finger painting, but he held the brush like he thought he might have to bash someone over the head with it. I had to stop and help him more than the seniors because he was color challenged.

"What do you get when you mix yellow and red?" I asked.

"Brown," he said confidently.

I tried not to laugh. I took my job seriously, even when I was getting paid less than minimum wage and covering the cost of supplies. My parents had never managed to climb their way up the career ladder, but one thing they taught me was to do my job with integrity, no matter what it was. For my dad, that was mopping the floors of office buildings, and for my mom, it was scheduling appointments for a dentist's office. Still, they showed me how to take pride in a job well done instead of what job was being done.

My dad always had a way of phrasing things that made them stick in my mind, and I still remember what he'd told me when I said I wanted to be an artist. He hadn't discouraged me or said there was no money in it. He'd thought for a while, took a deep breath, and nodded his head. "That's great. People are going to try to put that down, but those are the same ones who would put you down for wanting to be a plumber or a cook or a secretary. Do what you do well, and you'll never have to care what they say."

So when Ryan looked up at me with those dreamy, light

brown eyes, I looked back down to his palette and focused on the task. My dad would want me to remember my job was to teach art right now, and Ryan desperately needed to be taught.

"Actually, you get orange." Without thinking, I grabbed his hand and helped show him how to mix more in a circular motion instead of the choppy, aggressive cuts he was using. I pulled my hand off of his incredibly warm and wonderful skin as soon as I was done, feeling a wave of tingling prickles roll through me where my skin had been against his.

"Hm," he said. "I don't think I understood the technique there. Can you show me again?"

I almost swatted at him and giggled like an idiot, but I managed to suppress it as I turned around and squeezed my eyes shut. *Paris.* I chanted the word in my mind like a mantra. I'd been doing a perfectly fine job of avoiding men up until now. Bit by bit, I could feel myself fighting through the girly stupidity that was threatening to make me deaf and blind to reason and good sense.

"Are you going to teach the rest of us how to paint this shit?" barked Grammy. Her words came out a little slurred through Earl's teeth. "Or are you going to flirt with the little boy in the front all night?"

"Did you need help?" I asked. My voice was a tight squeak, but I pretended nothing was wrong.

"Yeah.' Her lips turned up in a wicked grin. "I forgot how French kissing works. Maybe you horn-dogs can show us?"

Earl, whose mouth was a sunken, puckered little hole without his teeth, burst into scratchy laughter punctuated by hacking coughs. The rest of my students didn't seem as amused, or they were oblivious—I couldn't tell.

When class was over, Ryan's painting somehow still looked like it had been finger-painted, even though I'd definitely seen him using a brush. It was, without a doubt, the worst painting I'd ever seen a grown adult produce. If Jackson Pollock had a baby with Picasso and the baby grew up to be a cocaine addict who painted with shaky withdrawal hands, it still would've been better than Ryan's work. He held it up and looked at it with a wrinkled forehead, then turned it and smiled a little. "Oh, it was upside down," he said.

"You can tell?" I asked, tilting my head.

"No, not really. You're lucky I'm not looking for an art *teacher*, because I didn't learn a thing."

I frowned. "None of my other students complained."

"I guess they didn't have as hard a time focusing on what you were saying instead of how you looked saying it."

I self-consciously ran my hands across my hair, immediately thinking I must've had something embarrassingly wrong the whole time.

"No. I'm saying it was nice watching you. I can tell you really care about all of this. I guess I forgot to actually listen, is all."

I grinned. "If you had listened and ended up with that painting, I'd fire myself."

"From a place this nice? No way. You can't give up this kind of gig."

"Hey. Watch it. I'm lucky to have this job. I'm doing something I love and getting paid for it."

A slow smile spread his lips. "I like that."

"You like what?"

"You're passionate. It's refreshing."

"And what about you? Is your passion taking art classes at a retirement home?"

He didn't answer me immediately. Instead, his eyes ran over me as he bit his lip a little and let it go in a way that made my knees feel like jelly.

Paris. Just think about Paris...

A change came over his face, as if an unpleasant thought occurred to him. In an instant, the heat and flirtation in his body language melted away and there was only friendliness and professionalism left, but no heat. "Actually, I'm passionate about two things. Running my business, and, well this is going to sound weird, but holidays."

"What's weird about that? Everybody likes holidays."

He shrugged in a self-conscious way that was endearing from such a gorgeous guy. "Maybe not quite as much as me."

I smirked. "Sorry. I'm having a little trouble imagining what it looks like for someone to be too into holidays. Caroling dressed as Santa? The person on the block who turns their house into Halloween Horror Nights? Or the guy who gives speeches about pilgrims and Native Americans before letting anyone take a bite at Thanksgiving?"

He rubbed the back of his neck and scrunched his face like he was trying to figure out how to answer that.

"What?" I laughed. "Don't tell me that's you..."

"I mean—I've never done the pilgrim thing. But I do think people miss the point of Thanksgiving."

"Oh no," said William, who poked his head in the door.

I jumped back from Ryan like I'd been caught doing something wrong.

"Am I too late? Is he already admitting what a geek he is?" William strolled into the room and frowned as he plucked Ryan's painting from his hands. "Jesus. You call yourself an art teacher? This looks like you made him swallow as much paint as he could and let him vomit it up on paper. Actually, it'd be generous to assume this came out of his mouth. Maybe he—"

"Thanks for the professional critique, William," interrupted Ryan. "I'll try really hard to do better next time."

"I've seen an elephant paint a better picture than this, come to think of it. True story, there's this place where—"

"We get it," Ryan said. He gave William a healthy glare that pretty clearly said "get lost," but William was either oblivious or didn't care.

"So," William moved around the room, running his hands idly over everything within reach as he walked. He picked up a paintbrush, ran a finger down its length, and then set it back down after some consideration. "I came in here and caught you two grinning at each other like some horny high school kids. Highly unusual. What happened to the Ryan I know?"

"We weren't—"

"Shh," William said. "You don't need to make excuses. We're all adults here. I'm just trying to figure out why my good friend here," he moved to Ryan's side and squeezed his shoulder. "Why my *good friend* is suddenly going googly eyes when he's normally Mr. Friendzone?"

"If you want to keep thinking of me as your good friend, maybe you can choose a better time to talk about this with me," Ryan said through tight lips.

"Oh. *Oh. Ohhhhh*," William winked. "Shit. I'm cockblocking right now, aren't I? I've always liked to think of myself as a... What's the opposite of a cockblock. A cockgate? No, that sounds like a scandal. A cockpass? A cock enabler?" He tapped his chin and wandered toward the door, muttering more options to himself as he left without so much as a goodbye.

Ryan shook his head. "Have you known him long enough that I don't need to apologize for that?"

"Yes, unfortunately. His grandma-in-law is one of my regular students."

"Well, I never did explain what I was looking for. I need someone to make posters and do some prop design kind of stuff for this Halloween thing I'm throwing. It's a big company party for everyone at my bakeries and at Galleon. It wouldn't be a big deal. Nothing too formal, but I wanted it to have a personal touch instead of buying something pre-made."

"How many people are we talking about here?"

"Well, I've got about thirty employees. And Galleon is a little bigger than my crew. So... Call it about two thousand and thirty people?"

I felt my eyes go wide, but tried to play it cool. "I see. And would I be working directly under you?"

"If that's how you like it," he said. There was a moment of silence as the corner of his mouth twitched up in amusement.

I felt my cheeks burning hot, but nodded my head. "Under you is good. I mean, any way would be good." I squeezed my eyes shut and lowered my head. "The job sounds good. Thank you."

2

RYAN

When Hailey put me in charge of The Bubbly Baker, I didn't quite know what to make of it. She'd found a new passion in her career cooking on TV, and she said I was the only one she could trust to run the bakery.

Of course, there was a slight catch.

The bakery she gave me was nothing but an idea at that point. The Bubbly Baker had been closed down and all she had left were a few regular customers and a recipe book. Basically, she crashed the car into the ditch, watched it burst into flames, and then handed me the keys.

It was a challenge. Lucky for her, I liked challenges. I also happened to like baking. So I'd rebuilt the company from the ground up with her husband, William, as my primary business partner, which was a scary concept. He loaned me the money I needed to get the business humming, and our business partnership thankfully started and stopped there. William Chamberson was also the dumbest genius I'd ever met, so tying my future to him was a little bit of a risky proposition.

The Bubbly Baker had three locations now. As it turned out, I was pretty damn good at finding ways to expand and grow the brand. William and Bruce had a tradition of throwing a company-wide Halloween party, and this year, I'd offered to organize it. I claimed to be so generous because I wanted to let my own employees get an invite, but the truth was I just loved anything that had to do with the holidays. The idea of a massive, high-budget Halloween party for a few thousand people sounded like it had the potential to be the most fantastic kick-off to the holidays I'd ever been a part of.

I lived for this time of year. For the heat of summer melting away, holiday music in grocery stores as soon as October rolled around, and every company putting out their Christmas themed commercials. I'd always been a nostalgia junkie, and there was no bigger hit than holidays. Crisp Fall nights brought me back to years of tacked-together costumes and sugar rushes with friends. It was the time of corny sweaters and crowded rooms filled with the smell of turkey and cranberry sauce. The icing on the cake was the thought of fresh powdered snow, a crackling fire, and some Christmas music humming over the radio in the morning.

Just thinking about it was my drug, and when the holidays came around, I had a tendency to go a little overboard. This would be the first year I'd have a massive budget for going overboard, and I was almost scared to see what kind of monstrosity of a party I would end up putting together with William's money.

It was only two weeks until the big day, and I could hardly wait.

I got dressed for the morning as quietly as I could. I lived in a two-bedroom apartment in downtown New York City. By New York standards, it was above average. By normal standards, it was probably more like a few closets jammed together. If that wasn't tight enough, I shared the space with my roommate, Steve.

Technically, I could afford to live somewhere much nicer by now, and without the roommate, but I knew the business was money-hungry. I had to keep feeding the beast if I wanted it to grow. If I wanted to pay William back for his investment and become financially independent, I needed to be smart with what I had, too. So for now, I lived on the cheap where I could.

I cracked the door open and found Steve tangled on the couch with the latest pseudo-model girlfriend in his never-ending line of short-lived relationships. He was competing for a roster spot in the NFL as a quarterback, a fact that seemed to earn him an endless stream of highly attractive New York women, most of whom were just looking to attach themselves to paychecks he might bring in if he ever made it in the league. If that bothered him, he never mentioned it.

Steve groaned and rubbed a hand through his hair, making the dirty blond mess of hair look a little crazier. He squinted and sat up against the armrest, then looked down at the girl sprawled across his lap with a confused expression.

"Jenna," I said. "You met her at trivia night. You like her because she has 'the best fake tits you've ever seen.'"

He raised his eyebrows, nodding slowly. "Jenna," he said, almost experimentally.

"Jenna," I confirmed.

"Huh?" she said, rolling her head to the side, which made her lose balance and flop to the floor.

Steve reached to catch her with comically slow reflexes, then winced. "Sorry, babe."

She was already snoring lightly.

"You really know how to pick them."

"Shit, man. At least I pick them. What are you working on now, your fourth year of celibacy? Should I buy you some fucking priest's robes? Wait," he said, a slow, very stoner-like grin spreading over his face. "I'd have to buy you *not-fucking* priest robes. Get it? Because—"

"Let your brain wake up before you try to make any more jokes. Please. And worry about your own dick. It's going to fall off if you keep sticking it in anything that moves."

"Correction. Anything that moves the way I like. I've got standards, man. And it's called a condom. You know, those things you never have to buy because you're too busy being best buddies with girls instead of doing the Lord's work and putting your dick in them."

"Maybe you should be the priest. That was inspiring."

"Damn right it was. But I'm being serious. I worry about you, dude. It's not healthy to waste the prime of your life like this—playing with dough balls all day and shit. You need a woman, and no—not another one who likes to vent about her boyfriend to you while she's not wearing makeup."

"Did it ever occur to you that I might have girlfriends and choose not to bring them around you for obvious reasons?" I didn't, of course, but he didn't need to know that.

He frowned. "You hiding women from me? Not cool. I let you meet all my girls."

"And what an honor that is." I gestured toward Jenna. "Nice to meet you, Jenna. This has been great. Steve is probably going to forget he's supposed to be with you tonight and pick up somebody new, but I'm sure you've been really special to him."

Jenna's quietly snoring form gave no sign of hearing me.

"Uh, no. Tonight is Taco Tuesday, and everybody knows you do *not* pick up a woman from Cinco De Mayo. Anyway, man. I'm just saying. Life is like a buffet, and it's all you can eat hot girls, all day, every day. Meanwhile, you're at the fucking salad bar poking tomatoes with your finger like a dweeb. Variety is the seasoning of life. You should try sprinkling some in. That's all I'm saying."

"It's the *spice* of life."

"Uh. Yeah. That's what I just said."

I shook my head. "I've got to get to work."

Steve sank back down on the couch and yawned. "You have fun with that."

He liked to act like he didn't work, but I knew he busted his ass studying videos of his practices and of the team, working out, and practicing. If you believed the analysts, he could've had a chance as a starter already, but in typical Steve fashion, he'd shot himself in the foot off-the-field, and not entirely in the figurative sense. He'd actually shot himself in the leg. An unlicensed firearm in his car had gone off while he was spinning it on his finger to show off for some girl. He was lucky it hit himself, and far luckier that no permanent damage was done.

His obvious lack of decision-making skills had slowed down the interest in him as a starter, despite his talent.

The plus side was his paycheck was pretty nice, and he always paid his rent on time. The downside was... well, there were a lot of them, but it was smarter to focus on the positives when it came to Steve.

I didn't work in the bakery as much lately. I spent most days out having meetings with people who needed to be convinced a Bubbly Baker franchise was exactly what they wanted and with the owners of my existing stores to keep them on track. I often wondered why I tried so hard to make the franchise huge. I'd never been the type to care much about money or success. I was happiest when my hands were dirty and I was making something I could be proud of. Yet here I was.

I'd told Emily from the nursing home to come here so I could explain what I'd need from her for the Halloween party. I had a startlingly clear image of her in my mind still: strawberry blonde hair, soft lips, and eyes that were just slightly wide-set and large in a way that made me think of a Disney princess. Then again, I'm not sure a Disney princess would ever wear paint-stained clothes and wear her hair as messy as Emily did.

I liked how she didn't seem to be the type to preen over herself and spend hours getting ready. I didn't feel like I was seeing a carefully crafted illusion when I looked at her. She was herself, and she was unapologetic about it. I started breathing a little faster just remembering how good it'd felt to have those playful, teasing blue eyes of hers on me. Worse, I still couldn't shake the feeling that I remembered her from somewhere.

I'd worked for so long in the city that she could have just been a customer who left an impression on me, but I felt the strangest connection to her that seemed to go deeper than some chance encounter could've managed.

I needed to calm that line of thought down, though. Way down. Even thinking of commitments and girlfriends brought up all sorts of ghosts from my past that I wasn't eager to confront.

STEPHANIE UNLOCKED THE DOOR FOR ME WHEN SHE SAW ME reaching for my keys at the shop. She let me in with a smile. She was definitely pretty, and I think when I first met her I'd probably thought of her as hot, even. Leave it to my screwed up brain to rewire itself until I could only think of her as a sister or a friend. It was like a defense mechanism, as if there was some cock-blocking monkey that lived inside my skull and immediately set to work reprogramming my thoughts if they steered toward romantic. *Can't have that kind of pain and disappointment again, can we?*

Everybody, especially Steve, liked to joke that I was gay—or a closeted 'sword crosser' in his words—but it wasn't that at all. Sometimes I got over-eager about setting women up with guys, but it was more because I worried if they stayed single long enough, I'd get it in my head that I might want to date them. I'd set Hailey up with William, and I'd tried and failed to set Stephanie up twice already. For some reason though, I couldn't picture myself trying to pass Emily off on some other guy. Even thinking of it stirred up a strong wave of jealousy and possessive-ness, which was ridiculous. I'd flirted with the woman for a few minutes and she'd smiled back at me. It wasn't like I'd gotten on one knee and said vows.

In a few days, I knew it'd feel different, anyway. The cock-blocking monkey was probably already working on making her romantically dead to me, even if I couldn't feel the flame of interest dulling yet.

Stephanie gave me a searching look as we headed to the back of the bakery, where she had a tray of dough out and was portioning it out for bread. She had brown, curly hair, blue eyes, a smear of freckles across her nose with an easy smile to match the *girl-your-parents-would-love-for-you-to-date* look.

"Hmmm," she said.

"What?"

"I've seen that look before. I'm just trying to remember when the last time was."

"You're imagining things, then. I don't have a look."

She planted a fist on her hip and gave me a very good impression of a sassy child movie star—the kind where the hip goes out, the eyebrows go up, and the lips purse into a tight knot. It was the kind of look that usually prompted the laugh track to kick in.

I grinned. "Stop doing that. You look ridiculous."

"So do you. And I know what it is, now. Those are lovesick eyes. You met somebody, but fate is trying to tear you apart." Her voice had become deadly serious, and her eyes were a little wide. Stephanie was very much in the hopeless romantic category, and I think she woke up every day dreaming that her life would magically turn into a romance novel where men with long, flowing hair always wait around the corner to rescue her from trouble.

"Definitely not." I picked up a handful of dough, weighed it, and started working it into a ball.

She got closer and sniffed. "Since when do you wear cologne to work?"

"I always do," I lied. "I must've just put too much on this morning."

"It's love." She stated it like she was passing down a terminal diagnosis. "I never thought I'd see the day. Ryan Pearson, the unflatterable, undateable, stone cold—"

"I get it." I wanted to snap at her, if only because the more she talked, the more she was convincing me that I really did feel some kind of budding romantic idea about Emily, who I hardly knew. I couldn't get upset though. Stephanie's goofy excitement had me smiling, even if I was terrified she was right on some level.

"When do I get to meet her?"

I grabbed another ball of dough and tried to ignore the question, but something wet and sticky collided with the side of my head a moment later. I peeled the dough from my face and looked incredulously at Stephanie, whose face was contorted in anger.

"You threw a dough ball at my head? Are you crazy?"

"When!" she demanded.

"Jesus Christ," I laughed. "You're serious?"

"Ryan. I've known you for like... four months. You're a great guy, but I've never even heard you talk about having a girlfriend. You pushed me away like you were the most loyal, married man on the planet—not that I was trying to get with you, or anything."

I smirked. "Of course not."

"What I'm saying is this is the *first* time I've seen you like this. We live in New York City, and you must see hundreds of girls every day. This one must be something super special to get you so excited."

"Okay. Pump the breaks. Nobody said I was 'super' excited. In fact, I haven't even confirmed a single thing you've said."

"You don't have to. If we were in a cartoon, your pupils would be little pink hearts right now."

"Well, we're not in a cartoon," I said it a little more shortly and forcefully than I intended, but all the wrong memories were bubbling to the surface. It only took so many horribly failed relationships before you had to look in the mirror and start to ask if you were the problem. Two girls in high school had cheated on me. One in college had broken up with me and decided she wasn't into men anymore. After college, I'd dated a girl who ended up throwing all my clothes outside and literally setting them on fire because she thought she'd caught me checking a girl out during lunch. Forget the fact that I hadn't been. The novel of my love life would be titled *Fifty Shades of Failed Relationships*. And it definitely wouldn't be a bestseller.

After the clothing bonfire, I'd finally had enough. No more women. Even if I'd wanted to, my brain had become exceptional at finding game-breaking flaws, usually where there were none. Everything turned into a red flag, and it became easier to pair off eligible women with other guys or think of them like sisters. Relationships that never happened couldn't fail, after all.

Emily came into the shop a little after lunch with a backpack slung over her shoulder. It was a typical artist's backpack. Multicolored paint was splattered on the army green fabric. She even had a little misting of white paint on her temple and cheek when she walked up to the counter and gave me a crooked little smile. Her dress was white and black, and it fit her in that perfect zone between revealing and modest that left my eyes hungry for more.

Just like the last time I saw her, I had that nagging sense of familiarity. I wanted to ask her about it, but worried she'd think I was being a creep for remembering her from some chance encounter. I made sure not to smile too wide back at her. I wasn't trying to win the girl over, anyway. I needed to remember the universal truth. Relationships and I don't get along, and no matter how nice Emily might seem at first sight, she'd inevitably self-destruct, just like they all had. I'd lost sight of that yesterday, but a little time apart had reminded me to keep perspective.

"Grab a table," I said. "I'll be over in just a second so we can talk specifics about the job."

"Sounds good." Her voice was chipper and everything in her body language said she was relaxed, but I noticed how restless her eyes were—darting from mine to my chest, to Stephanie in the back, and then to the ground. Knowing she was probably interested too was only making everything harder.

"Hey," I said to Stephanie, once I was in the back and out of ear-shot from Emily. "You're on your own for a little, I've got—"

"Oh. My. God." Stephanie slid to the corner and peeked out at Emily. She bit her lip and then turned to me with bulging eyes. "She is so freaking adorable. I want this. I *need* this. She's so perfect for you. Look at that outfit!" Stephanie gripped my shirt and shook me a little. "She's all covered in paint and grungy but still cute and peppy. *Go to her!*"

I shook my head, laughing softly. "I'm glad you approve of the artist I'm hiring in a purely professional context, for purely professional purposes."

Stephanie made a very serious face and nodded enthusiastically, then flashed me a wink. "Oh, absolutely. I totally understand. Completely."

"You're unbelievable."

"Yes! That's the line you should open with. Go right up to her and say it, but try to make it sound a little sweeter and a little less... Disgusted."

I walked over to Emily, making a conscious effort to ignore Stephanie, who was sticking her head out from the back with as much stealth as a dog who heard the crinkle of a bag of treats.

"You're late," I said as I pulled out a chair and sat across from her. It was only ten minutes past the time we'd agreed on, but one reason I'd had so much success getting The Bubbly Baker back up and running was my ability to judge character. I wanted to see if she was the type to make excuses or own up to her mistakes.

"I know. I'm sorry. It won't happen again. I'm kind of horrible with directions—more horrible than I realized, apparently. I'm going to just print out walking directions next time to wherever you need me to go and still leave fifteen minutes early. You know, in case I have them upside down or something." She was talking very fast, and she ended her sentence with a breathless, nervous little laugh.

Her lips had a way of curving upward as she spoke while her

eyes stayed lock-focused on mine. It had an arresting effect that made me realize how addicting her attention could become, and quickly.

I nodded. I liked her response. Truthful, with a touch of an excuse, but also with an explanation of why she wouldn't make the same mistake again. "Fair enough. So I was hoping you could get the posters ready by the end of this week, and everything else by the 30th. I have no idea what kind of timeframe these things usually have, but I can pay extra if that's too quick."

She looked down at the table, eyes searching the table top for a few seconds before she looked up to my eyes and nodded. I liked the determination I saw there. From the look on her face, I'd asked something that would stretch her abilities, but she was also up for the challenge.

The damn woman wasn't helping me out in the emotional distance category. The more I talked to her, the more I wanted to know about her.

"Supplies are on me, obviously," I added.

Her eyebrows twitched up at that, but she regained her composure quickly. She wasn't expecting me to offer to cover the cost of supplies? What kind of people had she been working for?

"I really appreciate this chance. I won't let you down." Her words sounded stiff, and she was having trouble meeting my eyes. I wanted to reach across the table and grip her hand, which I was surprised wasn't trembling from her body language. There was a strength and fire in her that was at odds with the way it looked like she was about to throw up from nerves. Go figure, I liked that too.

"Great." I grabbed a napkin out of the dispenser and slid it across the table to her and set down a pen. "Just write down what you'll need on here and I'll get it for you."

"Well, I've already got most of what I'd need," she said. She looked serious as she tapped the back of the pen between her teeth and chewed idly on it. Then she quickly jotted down some brands of paints, colors, and dimensions of the paper she'd need. She also added some kind of computer software and specs for what she'd need to print the posters. I thought she was done, but then she quickly scribbled something I couldn't quite read upside down and leaned back in her chair.

I slid the napkin to my side of the table and turned it upside down. At the bottom of the napkin, she'd written: "a workspace" in apologetically small, sloppy letters.

I hadn't thought of that. "You don't have space at your place?"

"Ever tried to paint in a closet? I can do it, but my place is already crammed with my own stuff. It'd be a lot easier if you had somewhere I could keep all the supplies and work." She waited for my response with a lopsided smile.

I ran a hand through my hair as I tried to work through my options. None of the bakeries would be a good space, unless I set up a canvas in the middle of the lobby. I couldn't ask her to come to my place, not with Steve... *Shit.*

"I'm sorry," she said. "I'm sure I could figure something out if—"

"No. no. It's okay. I have an idea. It's not a good one, but it's an idea."

EMILY WAS GOING TO COME TO MY APARTMENT TOMORROW afternoon. She'd left with a chipper, casual goodbye, and I had a lump in my throat. All my confidence that she'd end up just like every other woman of the last few years felt like it was evaporating. I wasn't so sure she'd gradually burn out of the romantic portion of my thoughts and into the platonic side.

Stephanie sighed dreamily at me when I came back behind the counter after Emily had left.

"Looking at you two was like magic. The tension. The chemistry. The suppressed emotion." She was talking through gritted teeth now and her fists were balled. "I was wondering if you were just going to leap across the table and *claim her*. Right then and there."

I grinned. "Maybe next time."

Stephanie punched my chest a little harder than I would've thought she could. "This is your problem. Fate is staring you in the face and you're just grunting and shrugging about it. *Do something.* Go get her. Sweep her off her feet. Give her a full-frontal romance!"

I grinned. "I just met the woman yesterday, and my problem is that I'm not giving her full-frontals?"

"*Of romance,*" she corrected.

"I don't know anything about her. She could have a boyfriend. Her favorite hobby could be drugs or taxidermy. Maybe she doesn't even like men."

Stephanie gave me an impatient look. "She was looking at you like a dog looks at a strip of bacon. Trust me, she likes men. And she likes *you*. And so what if you don't know anything about her? That's why you take her on a date. You talk. Let the sparks fly."

I leaned back against the prep table. I didn't want to have to come clean to Stephanie, but I didn't think she'd ease off unless I explained my reluctance. "I don't have the greatest history with relationships. I'd kind of prefer to keep things cordial and avoid the inevitable blow up that would come if things got serious between Emily and me."

"I have a newsflash for you. Every single person on the planet in a happy relationship didn't have the greatest history with relationships either. And then they found the one. That's the whole point. It won't work until it does, but you keep trying."

"I wish you didn't have a point."

She beamed. "So you'll do it?"

"Only to get you to get off my back about it. But there's no telling what she's even going to say, so don't get your hopes too high."

"Wow, just like that?" she asked. Her eyes were wide again

and she was leaning in like I was some kind of mysterious speci-men. "Shouldn't you at least be a little nervous to ask her on a date out of nowhere? What if she says no?"

I grinned. "First, you push me into doing this, and now you're trying to convince me I should be scared?"

"No, no. Not scared. You've got nothing to be worried about at all. I mean, look at you! I was just thinking it'd be really awkward if she *did* say no, since you two are kind of working together. That's all."

I looked at the napkin Emily had written supplies on and studied the phone number she'd left at the top. I hadn't asked for her number. Maybe it was some kind of subtle hint that she wanted to be asked. I probably should've felt nervous like Stephanie was saying, but now that I knew I was going to call, the overpowering emotion pulsing through me was excitement. That, and maybe a little bit of cold dread mixed in there—dread that I was setting myself up for the next disappointment in what had been a long line of disappointments.

3

EMILY

My apartment was kind of like what you might see on an episode of hoarders, except if the hoarder lived in a ninety square-foot apartment. It looked more like if somebody grabbed a random, small section of a hallway, covered it in brick, and slapped a dingy window on one end and a door on the other. For perspective, the walls were only one foot wider than my single mattress.

Oddly enough, I kind of liked the cramped living space. I knew where everything was, and I'd become very good at deciding exactly what was essential for my life and what I didn't need. It felt like my little hobbit hole. My escape from the bustle of the streets. It was cozy, even if I didn't really have room to work on my art projects like I'd have wanted. I found ways to work around it, like staying late at the retirement home and using their space.

I had no plans for the night, which meant I was deep into my *I'm-not-stepping-foot-out-of-the-house* wardrobe. I wore an over-sized, fuzzy cat-face sweater with sleeves that dangled over my hands. I'd shed my pants hours ago, and even if the police came to the door, those puppies weren't going back on. It was going to be that kind of night: the perfect kind.

My mind still traced over the memory of talking to Ryan in his shop a few hours earlier. Like idle fingers moving over something out of place, my mind revisited every word and phrase, every hint of body language and moment of eye contact. I knew Paris was more important than anything right now, but I also knew it was only October. Art school wasn't until January. Would it really be so bad to just have a little fun in the meantime? I mean, was I supposed to live like a nun for the next few months?

I wasn't doing a great job of convincing myself, though. Getting into a relationship now would be like adopting a puppy with a terminal illness. I'd only be setting myself up for heartbreak, no matter how much those puppy eyes and those bulging, perfectly sculpted biceps were making me want to pull the trigger. I shook my head at myself. My brain couldn't even keep the thought of Ryan and his biceps out of my puppy analogies.

I ran a longing eye over the posters on my wall. I had at least one from my favorite artists. I'd admittedly focused a little more on artists I might actually meet while I was in Paris, chief of which was Valeria Purgot. I fangirled over her hard enough that I'd actually sent a ridiculous letter with some samples of my work a few weeks ago. I liked to think it was subtle enough of a letter that it wasn't obvious I was basically begging to be her apprentice, but it was probably obvious. I cringed a little just thinking about how quickly she'd probably dismissed it and thrown it aside, if she'd even seen it.

I pulled an instant cup of hot chocolate out of the microwave and cradled it in my sleeves as I sunk down onto the bed and got back into my latest horror movie marathon. The city nightlife was just getting underway outside. In New York City, it started at sundown and didn't stop until sunup the next day, and I'd always found that invigorating and oddly comforting. It was like when I was a kid and I knew my parents were still awake downstairs while I slept. Some-body kept the light on. The reset switch never truly clicked, instead, the torch just passed from hand to hand and life rolled forward.

My phone rang. I half-heartedly checked the number, because the only people who called me at this hour were nurses confirming appointments or telemarketers. I considered hanging up when I saw the unknown number, but with my luck they'd leave a voicemail. A voicemail would join the two un-checked voicemails and stress me out for at least a week before I finally checked it.

"Hello?" I said into the phone. I popped a few stale pieces of popcorn into my mouth and waited for the inevitable, robotic recording to ask me if I was registered to vote, or if I'd been experiencing any unusual itching in my nether-regions.

"Emily?"

I almost choked. "Ryan?" I stammered, then coughed. "Sorry. I was expecting someone else."

"Oh. If you're busy I can call back at a better time."

"No!" I cleared my throat and made a gesture to myself to calm down before I sounded like even more of a freak. "Sorry. I'm just on edge. I've been watching horror movies all night. I'm not busy. What's up?"

There was a distinct pause, and I wondered if he was distracted, or trying to form the right words.

"I thought we should get to know each other a little better. We're going to be working together on this project, after all."

I chewed my lip and smiled. "How much are we going to be working together, exactly? I thought I was just making a poster and some props for you."

"I'll need to approve everything." His voice sounded a little defensive. It was cute.

"Oh, right." My eyes wandered past the TV to the desk where my acceptance letter to Paris sat. I pinned the phone to my ear with my shoulder and then made the sign of the cross at the letter. Responsibility could be damned, at least for a little while. "Maybe you're right. How do you suggest we get to know each other? Should we play an icebreaker game over the phone?"

"The phone won't work. I was thinking something in person. Tonight."

I sat up straight and took a despairing glance down at my outfit. "Tonight?"

"Sure. Why not?"

"No reason. What were you thinking?"

"You said you're watching horror movies? My roommate and his girlfriend are hogging the TV. Would I be an ass to invite myself over to watch some with you? I'm a huge horror movie buff."

I caught myself chewing my lip again and made myself stop. I needed to have some damn self-control if I was going to survive this thing and still make it to the airport in January. It was just temporary. Just a little fun. I had to remember that.

"Well, I could use something more sturdy than a pillow to hide behind during all the scary parts."

"Deal. I'll bring takeout and some beers. Or does wine sound better?"

"Beer is good."

"Perfect. I'm on my way." The phone clicked off and I looked at it in confusion. How was he on his way when he didn't even know my address?

It rang again a second later. I picked up with a knowing smile. "Forget something?" I asked.

"Yeah, where do you live, exactly?"

RYAN KNOCKED ON MY DOOR JUST OVER AN HOUR LATER. I MADE A few strategic moves with the time since getting off the phone. Move one was putting on pants. Next, I kicked all my dirty clothes and random bits of underwear into nooks and crevices where he wouldn't see them. After that, I spent a really long time perfecting the *I-didn't-spend-any-time-getting-ready,-I-just-always-look-his-well-put-together* look in the mirror. I opted to keep the oversized sweater on. It might not be the most flattering look, but if we were actually watching horror movies together, I needed my armor.

My heart was pattering away when I opened the door. I smiled in a way I hoped said, "Oh, hey, welcome to my crib. I wasn't expecting you, and this is exactly how me and everything in here always look."

He hoisted a six-pack of beers and the classic brown bag suspended in a white plastic bag that universally signified Chinese takeout. You knew it was serious to-go food when it needed two bags to be safely contained.

"I forgot to ask what you like, so I just kind of got a little bit of everything."

"Oh, don't even worry about it. I don't eat, anyway." I opened my mouth, frowned down at the floor, and then shook my head. "I mean, I eat. I eat all the time. Tons of food, actually. Human garbage disposal, practically." I pressed my lips together to stop the verbal diarrhea that seemed intent on flying out of my mouth.

When I'd been purposefully trying to keep things strictly North and South Korea with him, it had seemed easy. Now that I was starting to let my fantasies wander again, I'd apparently lost the ability to communicate like a normal human being around him.

He met my rambling with an easy smile. "It sounds like I don't need to worry about the food selection either way, then." Ryan paused for a moment to take in all of my apartment, and it literally was a second, because there wasn't that much to take in. I braced myself for a sarcastic or worried comment about how small it was, but he only moved beside the bed and set all the food down on the table beside it, which doubled as my kitchen table, drawing space, microwave food prep space, and sometimes as an extra surface for piling dirty clothes.

"I don't want to be presumptuous, but the table is facing the wrong way to watch TV. Does this mean we're eating in your bed together?"

"Is that weird?" I asked. "I hadn't even thought about it, but I could try to move the table or something."

"It's only weird if you make it weird."

"I promise, no weirdness from me, but I shotgun the wall side. I feel safer in the corner."

"Deal."

Ryan spread out the food across the bed on paper plates in a mini buffet and set two beers on the windowsill for me. It was probably highly unhygienic to be eating this much food in my bed, but I could always wash the comforter. Besides, it's not like I didn't already do it all the time.

My horror movie marathon was a self-composed collection of a combination between Netflix movies and movies I still had on DVD from the dark ages of my childhood.

I popped a piece of sweet and sour chicken in my mouth and turned the first movie on. *Scream.* "Hopefully you're okay with my selection, here," I said, "because you may have brought all the supplies, but I've been planning this movie night for *hours*. I had a very specific order in mind."

"Hey. I'm just here for an excuse to drink and eat junk food on a Wednesday. If I wasn't doing it next to a cute girl, it'd seem depressing instead of fun."

"Where is she and how'd you get her in here?"

"What?" he asked.

I swallowed and winced. Joke number one of the night sailed right over his head. "I was trying to say that I wasn't, well, nevermind."

He grinned. "I'm just messing with you. I got it. Seriously

though, you're cute. I like the whole artist look you have going on. You really pull it off."

I tried to think of something self-deprecating and charming to say. My muddled brain forced me to settle for a nervous laugh that sounded more like an asthmatic horse.

He burst out laughing at the sound.

I couldn't help grinning along like I was in on the joke. "That's not how I laugh. *Normally*."

Ryan's eyes seemed to twinkle as he looked at me and tried to control his laughter. "Well, it should be. I wish I had a recording of that noise. Having a bad day would be impossible. I'd just whip it out and listen to whatever that was on repeat."

"Whenever you're done teasing me, I was thinking about actually starting a movie. I have six hours of movies to get through tonight and work in the morning for my new boss, so I need to get this show on the road."

"New boss, huh? What's he like?"

I made a show of thinking hard. "Well, if he wasn't an ass who made fun of people for sounds they couldn't control, he'd be okay."

"Just okay? It sounds like you need to get to know him better." Ryan's eyes seemed to get heavier, and I felt the offer hanging in the air between us. He inched closer to me, and I knew I was seconds away from kissing him. Paris couldn't have been farther from my mind when I put my hand down on the bed and leaned in.

The intro credits for *Scream* blared through my apartment, making me jump back from Ryan like I was fifteen and my parents had just walked in on me with a pillow between my legs. *No. That never happened. Definitely not even one time after I saw my first Ryan Gosling movie.*

"Sorry," I blurted. "I saw an eyelash on your cheek. I was about to get it and then... *yeah*." I swiped my finger across his cheek and acted like I was brushing an eyelash away. "Got it."

"Right. Thanks. You had something on your lip. I was about to get it." His grin told me he knew exactly how full of crap I was, and then the way he slowly swiped his thumb across my bottom lip told me I still wasn't in the clear. "Got it," he said.

"Thanks." I stuffed a huge bite of crab rangoon in my mouth and stared at the TV like my life depended on it. I chewed while my lip still felt like it burned hot from where he'd touched it.

My mind wandered for the first half of the movie. I replayed the moment when my hand must've pressed play on the remote, and how easy it would've been to simply grab the remote, pause the movie, and resume where the two of us left off.

At the same time, I felt pulled in two directions. Part of me obviously wanted something to develop with Ryan, or I wouldn't have let tonight happen in the first place. Frustratingly, another part of me seemed to be running sabotage duty so I'd make it on my flight in January.

4

RYAN

"What do you mean, 'nothing happened?'" Stephanie demanded.

I shrugged. "It's not code. I mean we ate Chinese food on her bed. We watched three old horror movies, and she fell asleep during the last one. I cleaned all the stuff off her bed and I left. What was I supposed to do?"

"I don't know, woo her? Pour on some charm? Take off your shirt?"

I paused with a ball of dough in my hands and gave her an incredulous look. "Take off my shirt?"

"Yes! Something. You could've said it was getting too hot in there, or that you can't stand getting in bed with your shirt on. The awkward would evaporate as soon as your abs came out."

"Somehow I don't think a relationship that begins because of flashing my abs is going to be a very meaningful one."

She let out a long breath and hopped up to sit on the prep table. "You're right." She squeezed her hands into fists and groaned through her teeth. "Ugh! I just want this to happen. What if you screwed it up for us last night? I mean, you're *really* good at the whole friend zone thing. And nothing leads to the friend zone faster than a first date turned platonic."

"Messed it up for *us?* I didn't realize you were interested in her, too."

"So you are interested, then?"

"Of course I'm interested. She's cute, funny, artistic, and she has something about her. It's hard to put my finger on, but I like it. I feel good around her."

"So what's the holdup? Seal the deal!"

The hold up was the same as it always was, not that I was about to admit that to Stephanie. I liked Emily. Maybe even a lot. But if my history had taught me one thing, it was the fastest way to screw things up between us was to push past the friendship barrier. I'd still gone against my better judgment and planned to kiss her last night. Resisting her wasn't going to be like the girls from before. I wasn't so sure I could rely on my brain to automatically turn off my interest for her.

The real question was whether I actually wanted it to.

"Seal the deal?" I laughed. "Maybe it's more like a marathon than a sprint. Did you ever consider that? This isn't some movie where we have to fall in love in the first second of meeting each other. Real relationships take time."

"Ugh. Don't *real relationships* me. I want results. I want fireworks. And I want them now."

"Noted. You can put that in the suggestion box, if you want."

She slapped her palm on the black box hanging by the front counter. Dust blossomed upward from her hand. "This one?"

5

EMILY

Lilith parked outside Ryan's building. She gave me a long, suffering look, and then sighed so hard I thought she might pop a lung.

"What?" I laughed.

She looked at me in her typical Lilith way. Dark hair. Dark eyes. Darker expression. If a teenage girl had to listen to an endless loop of dad jokes in her head, they would make the face Lilith always made. If it wasn't for the faintest sense of almost feline enjoyment she tried very hard to hide, she'd be unbearable. Instead, I actually enjoyed her sour moods.

"If you think I'm going to ask about whatever it is that has you so excited, *I'm not,*" Lilith said.

"I'm not 'so excited.' I'm just grateful to have a little extra work."

She gave me a dry look. "And that's why you did your hair all fancy and you smell like unicorn barf?"

"Wait, is that bad?"

"If you're horny, just own it. Pretending it's something else makes it gross."

"Horny? It's just a job, Lilith. A job I'm happy to have."

"I've seen Ryan. When Hailey handed over the business to him, he used to come by Galleon all the time to meet with William. Even I'll admit he's hot. *Own it.* You're horny, and you're hoping he slaps you around with his big, fat cock, assuming he hasn't already."

"Lilith!" I laughed. "That's pretty specific. Are you sure this isn't your fantasy?"

She slowly slid her eyes over me and smirked in a way that made me uncomfortable. "My fantasy would start in a dark room. The air would be so cold my nipples could cut diamonds. He'd have a whip, and he'd be wearing a mask..."

I held up a hand. "Pretty sure I got the idea. Thanks."

"Are you going to admit it, or do I have to torture the truth out of you?"

"Admit what?"

She leaned forward, pulled my blouse forward, and looked down at my bra. She started reaching for my pants but I managed to slap her away.

"What the hell are you doing?" I snapped.

"Proving you dressed for a guy. Lacy black bra, and I bet you wore the panties to match. Admit it. *Harlot.*"

I clamped my mouth shut and pushed the door open. "As much fun as it is getting molested by you and your dead eyes, I've got some work to do. And who says harlot anymore?"

She reached forward and pulled at my pants just in time to laugh triumphantly. "A thong! You dirty little—"

"Okay, bye!" I said, slamming the door on her. Seeing Lilith laugh was a relatively rare sight, unless somebody was in pain or getting horribly embarrassed. Unfortunately, I think I was satisfying her on both counts, because I could see her shaking with laughter through the tinted windows of her car.

I waited for my cheeks to stop burning with embarrassment before I headed inside the building.

Ryan's apartment was on the first floor, just past the grungy lobby. It wasn't the high-class, fancy kind of place I'd expected a guy like him to live in. He owned several bakeries and dressed well, but I guess even a very wealthy person had to live modestly in the middle of the city. I actually relaxed a little when I saw just how modest the building was. When I thought I'd be walking into some sleek, modern bachelor pad, I'd been worried about how awkward I'd feel.

After all, he'd seen my cramped place already. I thought back on last night and wanted to crawl inside myself and hide under a blanket. Not only had I klutzed my way out of a kiss, but I'd also fallen asleep during *The Shining*. It wasn't my fault Ryan smelled so good, or made me feel so cozy and safe. And *maybe* I'd hardly watched any of the movies because I was too preoccupied with the fact that he was right there next to me, just radiating hotness like a space-heater.

It didn't help that I had no idea where we stood now. Were we "talking," "dating," "on the fast-track to engagement," or had we already moved to "tried it but it didn't work"? I stood outside his door and waited until I wasn't breathing so hard I'd freak him out and raised my knuckles to the door.

I knocked twice and waited. There was a loud thumping sound, a curse, and then a girlish giggle. I felt my expression darken as I stood and stared at the flaking brown paint on the door. When he'd said I could use his apartment to paint, he'd given me a key with instructions: knock twice and wait two minutes. Did he seriously tell me to wait because he wanted time to usher some girl out the window before I came in? Was he seriously trying to kiss me last night and now he's already fooling around with some harlot? *Damn it, Lilith.*

My teeth were clenched and my tongue was buzzing with a need to lash out and do some damage—anything to take away the sting of embarrassment I was feeling. But I had to tell myself to relax. I didn't have any claim over him. I didn't even have a right to be upset about having to work in his apartment, considering it had been my own problem that I needed a space to work. It was just something I'd have to swallow and deal with. At least it made the whole 'guys are a bad idea right now' part of this situation much easier to solve.

I opened the door at exactly two minutes. The first thing I saw was a half-naked woman in red panties with an oversized t-shirt. Her hair was a mess, but she was so pretty she managed to look like the movie version of women who just woke up, and not the version of just woke up I usually pulled: drool dried at the corner of my mouth, puffy eyes, hair like a tumbleweed, and quasi-moto posture.

I manufactured a smile and reached to shake her hand. "I'm just here for work," I said. I wanted to make sure she knew this wasn't going to turn into some catty fight over some guy. She could have him.

She raised her eyebrows. "Like... prostitute work?"

"What? No. *No.* Art. I do artwork." I straightened my back a little. *Technically, I teach senior citizens some art basics at a retirement home three days a week and take any scrap of work I can find in between.* She didn't need to know that, though.

"Oh. Did Steve hire you to paint me naked or something?" she wiggled her eyebrows and twirled her hair. "My right side is my best side, well, unless it's like, a really high angle. Then I'm actually probably prettiest from the right, but not too far to the right. My nose has this little ridge here—see it?"

"Wait, who's Steve?"

"Paint her like one of your French girls, Jack," said a man's voice I didn't recognize. I turned to see a shirtless guy with a mess of dirty blond hair leaning in the doorway. He looked like a male model and wore a cocky expression that said he knew it.

"Oh my God. I have the wrong apartment. I'm so sorry." I started back toward the door, hands fumbling for purchase on something—anything. I just wanted out of this situation so I could marinate in the embarrassment for the rest of my life. I knew something wasn't adding up in my head, but it wasn't clicking together in the chaos of the moment, like why the key Ryan gave me would work if I had the wrong place, but my brain was moving too fast to stop and figure out the whole picture.

The guy shrugged, crossing his arms. He had an athlete's build and glowing tan skin. Even though I knew I'd made nothing close to a commitment with Ryan, I felt like I needed to avert my eyes, just for posterity's sake. If this guy was the golden boy jock who had it all in high school, Ryan was more like the hot guy who inexplicably never ran with the "in" crowd. Even though he did. He had that slight edge factor to him, but he didn't wear it like a badge of honor. He carried a little cloud of mystery with him, while Steve looked like the type who might only be as deep as his tan.

"Considering Ryan has had a girl over exactly zero times since we've lived here, I'm thinking you probably do have the wrong apartment. But it looks like your key works, so..."

"You know Ryan?" I asked the floor.

"I'm his roommate, Steve." The guy walked closer and extended his hand with an easy smile. It was the kind of smile that made most girls do stupid things. For me, it was a little too cocky, too confident. I liked men with at least a touch of humility. *Like Ryan.*

"I'm Emily."

The half-naked girl shook my hand next. "Jenna," She gave me a cheerful smile. "Steve's going to be an NFL quarterback soon." She waited with raised brows, like I was supposed to faint or maybe pee my pants.

"I'm kind of badass," Steve said. He shrugged off his own statement like he somehow thought he was being modest.

"So... where exactly is Ryan? He said I could use his apartment to start working on a project for him, but I'm not seeing where I'd do that." I scanned the cramped living space. There was hardly room for much more than the couch, TV, and small kitchen, let alone a canvas. I honestly would be better off at my own place if this was the setup, but I guiltily knew I wasn't going to tell him that.

I turned when I heard loud footsteps from outside, like someone was running. The door swung open and Ryan was standing there, breathless and looking a little startled. "You're here," he breathed.

I gave a little shrug. I thought I did a pretty good job of making it look like I wasn't still feeling weird about last night. "Yep. Looks like you're the one who's late this time."

He frowned at Steve and Jenna. "Did you talk to her?"

Steve held his hands up. "No way, man. We've just been glaring at her since she walked in here. Why would we think of talking to her?"

Ryan pulled the front door shut and motioned for me to follow him. "Come on, I made some space in my bedroom."

"Oh shit," Steve muttered to Jenna. "I've never seen what his game with women is like. Apparently he goes for the shock and awe technique. The Blitzdick tactic. I thought it was a myth. Think he's going to show her his dick as soon as they close the door?"

"Definitely," Jenna said.

Ryan stopped just long enough to glower at the two of them. "Seriously? She's *working* for me. I don't even know where you get some of the idiotic things you say."

Well, I thought. *That clears that up.* If I had any illusions that he was thinking of me as some kind of budding girlfriend, I guess those ideas might as well hit the road.

Steve made sure we saw him winking and giving us the thumbs up as Ryan led me into the room.

Ryan shook his head. "Sorry about him. The two-minute wait was so I could have hopefully put a blanket over him and whatever girl he had in here before you came in, but it took me longer to get you all this stuff than I thought it would." He set down a handful of plastic bags that looked full of art supplies. "Honestly, I probably shouldn't have given you a key, but I wanted you to be able to come work whenever you needed, even if I wasn't here."

"It's okay. He was kind of funny."

There was a scuffling sound behind me from under the door. I turned and saw a "Magnum XL" condom slide under the door. At the same time, Steve whispered "*Blitzcock.*"

Ryan kicked it back under the door and gave me an apologetic look "If you just want to leave and pretend you never made the mistake of coming here, I'll understand."

"Nope. Sorry. You're stuck with me." I thought my words were obvious enough, but the silence that followed seemed to give them a deeper meaning. "Finding work as an artist is too hard to quit," I added.

"I'd say not when you're so talented, but I haven't actually seen you paint yet."

"Well, if you got everything on the list, that'll change in a few hours."

He hoisted the plastic bags from beside his door and dumped them on the bed. I nodded in approval as I looked through most of the supplies, but winced a little at the paints he'd picked up. I picked up one of the bottles. "This is actually oil paint. It's a nice brand, but I hardly ever paint with it, so..." I said slowly. "I feel like I'm being needy, but I really don't have the right kind of paper or brushes to use this."

"Then it sounds like we're going for another shopping trip. Why don't you come with me to make sure I get the right stuff this time?"

"Okay..." I had mixed feelings about the idea. On the one hand, I thought it'd be easy to keep this professional, even if I was using his apartment. I figured he'd show me the setup and leave me alone to work. On the other hand, going on a shopping trip with him sounded fun. To top it off, I'd get to physically pick out the high-quality paints I always dreamed of being able to afford.

For about the tenth time, I considered asking him if he remembered me from high school, but I thought better of it and settled for following behind him while he led me out. Everything that happened back then seemed less important with every passing hour I spent around him.

When we opened the door, Steve and Jenna were burning something in the kitchen and arguing over whose fault it was. Steve turned around and looked at Ryan. "Shit. The "blitz" part of blitzcock was supposed to be how quickly you whipped out the big gun, not how quickly you finished."

"We're going shopping," Ryan said.

"Shopping..." Steve scratched his bare, muscular stomach with the plastic spatula he was holding. "I don't know if I've ever tried that one. Hey, if he's having trouble getting it up, show him some classic holiday movies. He'll jump your jimmies in no time if you get him hyped up on holidays. Whisper "I'll Deck The Halls" in his ear or something. Or maybe ask if he wants to stuff your turkey."

"Yeah," Jenna said seriously. "The turkey one is better. Classier," she added with a little shrug.

I looked to Ryan for some kind of clue on how I was supposed to respond, but he only took my hand and pulled me through the living room and to the door.

He waited until we were a few steps away from the door to say anything. "Sorry about him."

"You don't have to apologize. My best friend is a sociopath, so I don't have any room to judge your choice of company."

"I'd assume you were exaggerating if I hadn't met Lilith before."

"She's an acquired taste."

"Maybe chlorine is too, but you wouldn't survive drinking enough to find out."

I grinned. "She's not that bad."

"The first time I met her, she literally hissed at me because I tried to shake her hand."

"She does do that sometimes... She's just trying to, kind of assert dominance? Okay, it actually sounds like she is that bad when I try to explain it out loud. Deep down though, she's really sweet."

Ryan and I walked a few blocks toward the nearest art supply store. He slowed and scanned the menu of a posh little gastropub as we were passing it and then checked the time on his phone. "I'm actually kind of starving. Do you mind if we get something to eat?"

I looked at the menu and saw the cheapest entre was over fifteen dollars. I was about to make an excuse that hopefully didn't make me sound too obviously poor, even though I'm sure he already knew.

"I'll get it," he said quickly "You're on the clock right now, anyway. The least I can do is pick up the tab for your lunch."

"It's okay, really. I don't want things to get complicated."

He raised an eyebrow. "You might be right. It could even be more complicated than trying to figure out if you're a badass for falling asleep during the scariest part of the shining, or if I'm just that boring."

"No, you weren't boring at all. Believe it or not, I haven't exactly been a hot commodity in the male community for a while. So if we'd played Monopoly, it would've still been the most exciting date I'd been on in years."

"So it was a date, in your mind."

"Oh, no. Definitely not. I mean, unless it was to you."

"Of course not. If we started dating, people would think I only gave you this job because I liked you."

"I didn't realize this was such a publically followed position."

He grinned. "It's not. Not exactly, at least. So, long story short, I think we could afford to have a little lunch together, and you could afford to let me pick up the tab. You did say something about being a starving artist, didn't you?"

"All joking aside, I think it'd be easiest if I just go ahead and put this out there. I have to leave for Paris in January. I got accepted to art school over there, and I can't let anything stop me from going."

"Wow." Ryan reeled back and seemed to mull that over a bit as he nodded to himself. "Well, I'm a Libra, I'm allergic to latex, and one time I went too deep at the beach while trying to body surf and almost drowned." He gave me a confused look. "What? I thought we were sharing random, irrelevant facts about ourselves."

I slapped his arm, grinning. "Ass. You know what I'm saying. Don't pretend you don't."

"Maybe I do, but It's only a date if we enjoy ourselves. So I promise, I'll be as boring as I can. Maybe I can even go two for two on getting you to fall asleep."

"I'm pretty sure that's not how it works. I've been on plenty of dates that were miserable."

"Oh? When was the last time?"

I checked the imaginary watch on my wrist. "What time is it?"

He smirked. "I like it. Sassy and sarcastic looks good on you."

"Stop trying to charm me. This was supposed to be a boring, unenjoyable not-date."

"It's not a not-date until we step inside." He yanked open the front door and gestured for me to go inside. "After you."

6

RYAN

Emily sat next to me at the bar. The place had a nice atmosphere that really fit the whole gastropub theme, down to the beer barrel barstools and rough wooden bar. Emily tucked her hair behind her ear as she looked over the menu. I liked her ears. They stuck out a little, and I could imagine they were the kind of feature a girl would probably obsess over as a flaw. To me, they were the kind of endearing physical trait I could imagine falling in love with—if I wasn't so sure my brain was going to step in and shut down all these feelings before long.

Then again, I also was feeling less sure my brain would save me from what I was feeling by the minute. I didn't seem to be able to stop singling out obscure little things about her and deciding they were exactly right, even down to the way she had a habit of rocking on the side of one of her feet when she was nervous, or the way she seemed to be nervous any time she was talking to me.

She was running her finger up and down the same few menu items. They were the cheapest options on the limited menu.

I leaned over and nudged her. "I'd tell you not to worry about the price, but this is supposed to be a shitty date, right?"

"Right," she said. There was a flicker of mischief in her eyes. "I'd also ask you why we're having drinks this early in the day, but by the rules of the horrible date, you're probably just an alcoholic."

"A raging alcoholic, thank you very much. And you'd better ask them if they serve half-sized portions, and don't even think about adding any extras. You'll be drinking water, too."

"Do I get to be shitty, too, or is it only a shitty date because you're being a jerk?"

"The suckiness needs to be reciprocal, for sure."

She raised an eyebrow at me.

I gulped at my choice of phrasing, and for the first time in as long as I could remember, I thought I might be blushing a little.

"No sucking on the first date, sorry," she said smoothly. Then, as if she was replaying her words in her head, her eyes widened slightly and she took a huge gulp of water.

"Deal-breaker," I said quickly, hoping to distract her. "I expect oral at least two times a day, and I also expect to never have to reciprocate. So, yeah, this isn't going to work."

She grinned. "No. You don't get to tell *me* it's not going to work, because I'm actually a hyper-vegan, and there's absolutely nothing on this menu I can eat. I can't believe you brought me to this place."

"A hyper vegan?" I asked, slipping out of my role as the horrible date for a moment as pure curiosity took over.

She looked up, clearly formulating some mixture of bullshit. "I only eat lab-grown meat and free-range vegetables. Zucchinis need just as much freedom as animals, and if they're surrounded by a fence, what kind of life is that? How can I support that?"

"You could do what I do. Refuse to eat any phallically suggestive fruits or vegetables, you know, because of the implication."

"Very mature."

"You made up the hyper-vegan thing, by the way, right?"

She crossed her arms and gave me a deadly serious look. "Why would I make something like that up?"

"Wait, you're serious? There's no way the Chinese we had yesterday was--"

She pressed her lips together to try to suppress a smile, but failed.

I sighed. "You had me scared for a minute there. This was about to take a turn for a real bad date instead of a pretend one."

"Hold on. If we're just pretending it's a bad date, does that mean it's actually a good date?"

I pressed my fingers to my temples. "This is the reason I didn't like that *Inception* movie. You're losing me here."

"I'm just trying to say, all jokes aside, that it's really not a good time for me to get involved with a guy. It's not anything personal, but I don't want to send the wrong messages."

Too late. "Yeah, I'm not trying to get involved with a guy right now either." I took a sip of my beer and then looked sideways to see her grinning at me.

"I'm being serious, Ryan."

"Me too. I don't judge, but that's not for me."

Emily looked toward the front doors and frowned. Two men wearing ski masks were moving toward the front counter. They both held a hand inside their jacket pockets. One stepped forward and pointed to the server near the register. "Empty it," he said coldly.

Time slowed down. I heard my heart pounding in my ears. My breath felt ragged, and my fingertips dug into my palms. It felt like a split second had passed since I was having a fun back-and-forth with Emily, and now I was in the middle of the scenario every man alive has spent countless hours mentally rehearsing: *How would I stop somebody if they came in here with a gun?*

In my head, the answer was usually some sort of crazy, bull-rush tackle that would catch a gunman off-guard, but here there were two guys and possibly two guns. More importantly, Emily was seated between the men and me. I slowly shifted my body so I was covering Emily as much as I could and gestured for her to stay calm. I felt her hug herself tightly to my back and press her cheek between my shoulder blades. Even with my heart pounding and my brain pumping me full of adrenaline, I took a moment to think about how good she felt wrapped around me like that.

I scanned the room for anything I could use as a weapon and started forming a plan. I wouldn't act first, because most robberies were non-violent, as long as the robbers got what they came for. At least I was pretty sure I wasn't making that up.

But if things turned bad, I thought I could upend a barstool and launch it at the guy closest to me and then get in to wrestle the gun away from the other one. Nobody in the restaurant was moving a muscle, which was good.

The cashier shakily reached to hand over a twenty dollar bill.

"That's all you have in there?" asked one of the men.

I frowned when I heard the voice again. It sounded familiar, but I couldn't immediately put my finger on whose voice it reminded me of.

One of the robbers nudged the other and pointed to me. "We've got a loverboy over here. Let's see if he's man enough to protect his woman."

There was something beyond cruel mockery in the words. They sounded almost faked, like somebody was doing a poor acting job of repeating a line they'd prepared to deliver ahead of time.

Both men turned to face us. I gripped the neck of my beer bottle tighter and mentally rehearsed what I'd do: bash the closest one over the head, rush the other. Maybe turn the barstool over and grab Emily so we could make a run for it.

The first man reached for me just as Emily let loose a sound I could only describe as a war cry. A half-full glass of beer shattered against one of the men's heads. I was startled, but managed to tackle the other one before he could react. I turned around and motioned for Emily to go out the back. "Go that way, call the cops."

She hesitated.

"Go!" I repeated.

The bartender was already pulling out his phone to call for help while everyone else scrambled to exit. I pulled my fist back to punch the guy I was pinning down if he tried anything, but when I yanked his ski mask off I felt my hand go limp.

"Steve?" I asked.

He flashed a confident smile despite being on his back and pinned to the ground. "Before you get mad, this wasn't my idea."

"Too late. I'm already mad. I knew you were stupid, but robbing a store? Are you absolutely insane? And what was with the loverboy shit?"

"Dude." Steve slid his hand out from under his jacket and made a finger gun at me. "No guns. And..." He pointed to the other masked robber, who was rubbing his head. "He's going to pay the guy off, so we'll be square."

The other robber pulled off his paint-soaked ski mask and grinned at me from beneath an impressive welt on his forehead. William goddamn Chamberson. He winked, then turned to the bartender. "Five grand if you forget this ever happened," William said.

The bartender looked at his phone and paused. "Cash?" he asked.

William dug out a wad of money rolled up like some kind of drug dealer and lobbed it at the man. "Yep. I hope you understand, but my colleague and I kind of have to run. *Now*," he added, punching Steve in the shoulder.

"Wait," I said. "What the hell was the point of all this?" I wished I could say I was totally shocked, but it wasn't the first time William had pulled some kind of grand prank on me. The man had too much money and time on his hands. Apparently, becoming a business partner had added me to the pool of available prank targets, in his mind. Steve being involved was new, though. On his own, Steve didn't have enough brain cells to rub together to think up a prank that went far beyond a whoopee cushion.

"Why do you think I told you about some random artist at my grandma-in-law's retirement home when you said you needed someone? You set me up with Hailey. Now it's my turn to set you up with someone. You two are perfect for each other, and I read this article once that said people form really strong bonds in life or death situations." He pulled Steve to his feet and jogged toward the door. "You're welcome!" he shouted over his shoulder.

"For what? I'm telling her this was bullshit."

"Wouldn't do that." William stopped at the door and turned around. "Think she'll believe you didn't have anything to do with it? Face it. You thought I was a cockblocker, but I've just set you up with the ultimate cockgate. Walk on through, buddy. You're trapped. You have no choice but to accept my expert matchmaking help." He gave a fancy bow and then started to sprint out the door, but his foot caught on the ledge and sent him rolling to the ground. He got up, shook it off, and ran out of sight.

Emily came back breathlessly a minute later. "Where are they?"

I glanced toward the bartender, who was making no secret about counting the huge stack of money William had given him. I led Emily outside as quickly as I could so she wouldn't see him or risk any of the people who'd run out to come back in and ask questions.

"They got away," I said quietly once we were outside. I thought about telling her right then and there. She knew William, at least a little bit, and anyone who knew him would know this plan was exactly the kind of idiotic scheme he'd dream up. It even had his annoying trademark hint of genius, because the more I thought about it, the more I realized he was right. Emily would think I was the most pathetic man in the world if she even suspected I'd put William up to something like this. It would look like I'd tried to force my way into a date, failed to ignite a spark, and now I wanted to resort to the lowest methods possible to manufacture one.

I was damned if I told her and damned if I didn't. I wished I could throttle William and Steve.

"I can't believe I just ran out like that. You said go call and I did it without thinking." She was speaking quietly and searching the ground like it held answers.

"I told you to. I didn't want one of them getting the idea to take you as a hostage or something." I cringed. I was just trying to make her feel better, but now it sounded like I was playing up my own heroics. "You know, I think they could've clocked that paint bottle at eighty miles an hour. At least," I added with a grin. "If painting doesn't work out, you could probably make a run for the MLB."

She laughed. "As soon as they replace baseballs with beer glasses, maybe." The humor drained from her face and she frowned down at the sidewalk. It was obvious that she was trying to come to terms with what had just happened.

The need to tell her the truth was overwhelming, but I'd already played along, and I wasn't innocent of the mess anymore, not completely. I wanted to growl with frustration, but I just put my hand on her shoulder and pulled her into a hug instead.

I was making a mistake. I knew it with a sinking, horrible feeling, but I also knew I couldn't stop myself from going along with it. I'd find a way to dissolve this, or a time to come clean. A better time. After a few days, it probably would be something we could laugh about. *Maybe.*

"It'll be fine," I said. "Besides, what are the chances of something like that happening twice? Plenty of people get caught up in a robbery once, but how many people have you heard of being bystanders in *two* robberies? You're practically immune now."

She laughed softly. "Comforting."

"Well, let's go get the right paints and cross our fingers that nobody plans to rob the art supply store."

I PACED IN FRONT OF WILLIAM'S DESK. I'D MADE STEVE COME TOO. Both men were looking up at me from their chairs with amused expressions, which only pissed me off more.

"In what world was any of that a good idea to you two?" I asked.

"Ryan," William was speaking in an infuriatingly calm voice, like he was trying to calm down a wild animal. "If it weren't for you, I might have never invited Hailey to that party. Because of you, I have my wife. That means I'm going to help you find your wife, whether you like it or not. Also, I've always thought I'd make a badass criminal. This was really a win-win situation, no matter how you look at it."

"Yeah," agreed Steve, who honestly looked a little confused about the reasoning but was excited to be on-board anyway. "Win-win, dude. Think about it."

"I refuse your help. Both of you. I don't want it. Okay?"

William shook his head and templed his fingers. "You don't get it, Ryan. This isn't about *you*. It's about what you need."

"What? That doesn't even—"

"You need a woman. And you need my help, because I've seen what you do. You friendzone anything with boobs. You're challenged in the dating department, and lucky for you, Steve and I are gifted."

"Prodigies," agreed Steve.

"Steve," I said. "If I wanted to learn the quantity over quality dating method, I'd check with you first. And William, you said it yourself, if it wasn't for me, you wouldn't be married."

William looked to Steve and shared a knowing smile with him. "He thinks he has a say in this. It's kind of cute, isn't it?"

"Adorable."

"Enough with the bad cop/stupid cop routine," I groaned. "I'm being serious."

"Wait," Steve said. "Which one of us is the stupid one?"

"Maybe the one who just tagged along because he was promised free beer?" William asked.

"I want both of you to swear this is done. No more weird fake robberies. Understand?"

Steve looked to William, then both men gave me a nod and a wink.

"No more robberies," William said. "I swear it on my brother's life."

"Swear it on something you care about," I said.

William looked aghast. "How *dare* you? I care about my brother. If something happened to him, do you have any idea how much harder I'd have to work? Besides, pissing him off is like a little ray of sunshine in my day."

"Fine. Steve?"

"I have to swear on something?"

"No. Just tell me it's over."

"Yep. Sure. No more robberies. You got it."

7

EMILY

L ilith sat on the edge of my bed in my apartment. It was the morning after those men tried to rob the gastropub, which already felt like a weird, half-remembered nightmare. I hardly ever had her over—or anyone, for that matter, but I'd called an emergency meeting and invited all of my friends. Lilith—A.K.A. "all of my friends"—sat with her black-nailed fingers on her knees, a look of hunger in her eyes.

"Did you see their guns?" she asked. None of her usual disinterest stained her words. I had her full and undivided attention, for once.

"No. They just had their hands in their pockets, but it was pretty obvious what they were holding."

"*Fuck,* yes," she breathed. "They could've shot you. Killed you. Right there, on the spot. Brain matter everywhere. Blood. It could've been a massacre. They would've had to do that crime scene thing with the red strings and the pins. Blood spatter analysis."

"Exactly what I was thinking," I said.

"What did you do?"

"I threw a bottle of paint at one of their heads."

Her eyebrows climbed her forehead. "*You?*"

"What? You don't think I have a little action hero in me when the moment arises? I used to watch every single Steven Seagal movie with my dad when I was a kid. Jackie Chan, too. I think I know what to do in any given kung foo scenario. I know how to bring down a perp with a pool cue. I also know if you kick somebody in the chest, white powder will inexplicably fly away from the impact. So yeah, you could say I'm an expert. *In theory, at least.*"

"Guns aren't kung foo, Emily."

"Well, a paint bottle to the head seemed to do the trick, even if I felt like I was about to pee myself. And Ryan tackled the other guy. So it worked out, anyway."

"Wait. You made the first move? Not him?"

"He didn't really have a chance. It just happened. They turned to look at us, and, well. It just happened. Boom. Beer glass to the head.."

"Light beer or normal?"

"What?"

"It matters."

"Normal?"

She nodded her approval. "Hardcore."

I grinned. "Maybe it sounds that way, but it was honestly pretty terrifying."

"Then why are you smiling?"

"Because it was kind of sexy seeing the way he put himself between me and the bad guys. And the way he jumped in to tackle the other one and took charge. *And* I'm kind of proud of myself for going all kung foo on them."

"Ugh." Lilith made a disgusted sound. "He was just thinking with his dick. Don't go giving him a medal over it."

"Wouldn't thinking with his dick be more like, I don't know, trying to do me in the middle of the action? I'd like to think he was thinking with his heart."

"Men's dicks are highly evolved thinking machines. It's not limited to immediate gratification. If a dick brain thinks it needs to lay the groundwork to get what it wants, it'll lay the groundwork. Believe that."

"I think you're giving penises way too much credit," I said. "And what makes you an expert? The last time I saw you with a guy was when you had that fling with the gothy barista."

"Just because I don't update my relationship status on Facebook or post pictures on Instagram, it doesn't mean I'm single. Ugh." She crossed her arms and looked to the side, but her annoyance looked a little more forced than usual.

"Let's assume I accept your penis brain theory. Is it the worst thing in the world if Ryan *does* want to get in my pants? Maybe these little britches haven't been cracked open in a few years too many."

She planted her palm on her forehead and closed her eyes. "One: never say britches again or do whatever that voice was. You sounded like Elmer Fudd with his balls in a vice. Two: I didn't need to know how long it'd been since you've boned a guy."

I cleared my throat. "Well, I'm so glad I called this little emergency meeting. You've been so helpful, as always."

Lilith stood and fixed her half-lidded eyes on me. "Emily, you have art school in January. Do you really want to get attached to a guy right now?"

She swept out of my apartment and closed the door, so I had nothing to do but mull over the question she'd asked, which happened to be the same one I'd been grappling with since yesterday.

Did I really want this?

RYAN MET ME OUTSIDE GALLEON ENTERPRISES. HE WAS WEARING A simple black t-shirt and gray shorts, all of which were covered in what looked like flour. His shirt had a little "The Bubbly Baker" logo. I smiled, looking him up and down.

"Cute," I said.

He smirked. "Your outfit isn't bad, either. What is that, a jean dress? It's cool."

I did a little curtsey and hoped I wasn't blushing. I shouldn't have been as flattered as I was by the compliment, but I always loved this dress. It just felt so... *me*. I liked that he'd noticed. I also liked the way he complimented me every time we were together. He didn't make it weird or make me feel like he was trying to get something out of it. He had a way of casually blurting the compliments like they just occurred to him and slipped out.

"Welcome to Galleon." He gestured to the huge skyscraper we stood beneath, where men in suits and women in pencil skirts bustled in and out.

"Do I get to know why I'm here and why you told me to bring my art supplies yet? Are we going to graffiti William's office or something?"

"As much as I like that idea, no. I think he might take back his offer if we did that. William heard about our little lack of space problem and said you could use one of the conference rooms on his floor to work. He had the room cleared of anything that'd get in your way. The only catch is, well, William. But he's probably going to be too busy working to really mess with you much."

"Oh." I smiled, but inside I was deflating a little. Working here meant I wouldn't have an excuse to see Ryan as much, and I wondered if I'd done something wrong to make him want more distance. I knew Lilith had a point in asking if I really wanted to be messing with a guy right now, but I also knew my heart fluttered and my skin prickled every time Ryan smiled at me. Couldn't I have the best of both worlds? I could let things play out between us and enjoy the holidays, and then maybe we could part on good terms in January when it was time for me to leave. We were both adults, right? As long as he knew our relationship would have an expiration date from the get-go, there'd be no hard feelings.

"Bad idea?" he asked.

"No, no. It's absolutely amazing. I was just wondering if I'll get tackled going through the door looking like this. I feel a little underdressed."

"Looking like that, *I* might tackle you. They won't." He smiled, but his expression fell when he seemed to realize what he'd said.

"As appealing as that sounds, I saw you tackle the robber yesterday. No offense, but I don't feel like getting a concussion."

"Oh, if I tackled you, it'd be much gentler."

I raised an eyebrow.

"Maybe it'd be best if I just stopped talking," he said.

"How else would you keep digging yourself in that lovely little hole?"

"Sorry, I couldn't tell if our date yesterday was a bad one or a good one, so I think I'm still not sure if I'm allowed to joke about tackling you, or if that's a no-fly zone."

"Oh, well, being witness to a robbery and throwing a glass bottle at a guy's head has always been really high on my top ten fantasies list. You completely failed at making it a bad date."

"Damn it. I guess you'll have to give me another shot. I promise, you'll hate the next one. Also, you're going to have to tell me the other nine items on your fantasy list. You can't just tease something like that and leave me hanging."

I gave him a little grin. "I'm taking the list to my grave."

"Hm," he said. "We'll see about that. Won't we?" He pulled open the front door for me and raised his eyebrows a little mischievously.

Inside, we passed the reception desk, where a pair of women with sleek ponytails and stylish black dresses were checking ID badges. I tried to wrap my head around the fact that William Chamberson was one half of the leadership of this entire empire and couldn't quite manage it. The only version of him I'd seen was the carefree, wild man who liked to cause chaos at the retirement home and tease his wife. I figured his much more grounded brother, Bruce, must have been the bigger factor in their meteoric success.

We waited for an elevator together and took the first one that dinged. Ryan pressed the button for the thirty-fourth floor and waited. A few men and women filed in and out as we rose up through the building. The elevator stopped almost every floor as people came and went, never quite leaving us alone until the fourteenth floor. The doors closed, and we were alone in the elevator.

Almost as if on cue, the lights flickered. Something heavy and mechanical clicked above us. The elevator rumbled, then lurched to an abrupt stop.

I frowned at the control panel where all the lights were blinking wildly.

"Oh God," I pressed my back to the wall and looked around. "I saw a horror movie where this happened once. The lights turned off and then there was this devil girl standing in the corner and she ate off some guy's feet. *Oh, God.*"

Ryan smiled confidently. "Hey, it's fine. I'm sure it's just some kind of power surge. And it's not like nobody knows we're in here. We just need to sit tight for a little bit and—"

"Actually," a voice said over the intercom in the elevator. "This is, uh, Fred—with the fire department. The elevator division. We're not going to be able to break you out of there. You'll have to use the hatch on the top and climb out yourselves."

Ryan glared at the intercom. "Fred, from the fire department? The elevator division."

"That's correct, sir. And I'll be honest, here. The only way you're getting that woman out of this is through some serious act of heroism. We usually try to do that sort of thing ourselves, but our hands are really tied here. See, there's been a, uh, labor dispute. Kind of like a sit-in." The voice on the intercom grunted, then muttered something I couldn't quite make out. "A walk-off, I mean. They're on strike, so it's just me here at the fire station, and the guys didn't even leave me the keys to the truck, believe it or not."

"What?" I said, more to myself than to anyone else. I was struck by the same feeling of odd unreality, like during the robbery. It was almost as if the man on the intercom was acting in some Bollywood movie and doing a terrible job of it.

Ryan put his hands on the wall and leaned close to the intercom. He whispered something so quiet I couldn't make it out.

"Nope." The voice over the intercom said. "I have no idea what you're talking about, sir. You'll need to climb out the top of the elevator. Heroism and all that. Thank you for your compliance."

Ryan punched the intercom button in. "Open. The. Door."

There was a weird edge to the fireman's tone. It almost seemed dismissive. I would've expected someone in his position to sound like he was trying to keep us calm. If anything, all he'd managed to do was piss Ryan off, so I decided to try my own hand at calming him down.

"Ryan, come on. I'm sure they would if they could. I think if you boost me up there, we can get to the top of the elevator. I've seen them do this on movies and *always* wished I could try it."

He was breathing heavily, and he looked back to the intercom one last time like he might punch a dent in the thing for good measure. "You're right. How hard could this be, anyway?"

He knelt down and threaded his fingers together to make a pocket for me to step into. I put my foot down and tested his ability to hold me up. His arms didn't even seem to strain against my weight. "Wow. You're strong," I said. I wanted to smack myself in the forehead as soon as the words left my mouth. I was one step away from clapping my hands together and chanting "Hercules, Hercules!"

"Okay, just let me kind of raise you up slowly. Don't jump or anything."

I nodded, sticking my hands up over my head and reaching for the panel at the top of the elevator. I didn't see any obvious way to open it, other than the square outline of a seam I figured you must be able to push and release. He raised me up, inch by inch, until I was able to put my palms against the cool metal roof. I pushed and strained. "It's not budging," I said.

"Shit. Okay. Try just putting your palms up flat and I'll give you a little boost."

"You mean you'll use me like a battering ram?"

"No. Well, yes. But carefully."

I swallowed hard. "Let's ram this bitch! *Carefully*," I added.

He laughed. "I like the enthusiasm. On three. One, two, thr—"

I felt myself rise up toward the ceiling far faster than I expected, and my arms immediately buckled under the sudden force of impact with the ceiling. My forehead collided with the ceiling, and then black clouded my vision.

8

RYAN

I'd ruined relationships in more ways than I could count, but homicide was a first. Emily was lying on her back with her lips parted and her body totally limp.

I patted her cheek and shook her softly. "Emily! Wake up!"

I checked her pulse and breathing. She was still alive, but she wasn't moving. I'd completely underestimated how fast and hard I could lift her up. And if I hadn't taken the world title of biggest idiot in that moment, I was at least in the top ten.

The elevator doors opened and William came in. He was bent over from laughing so hard, and he was wearing a ridiculous little plastic fireman's hat to go with his suit.

"Oh my God," he said through bursts of laughter. "I completely forgot they sealed those hatches when the safety codes changed. You just catapulted your girlfriend into a solid ceiling." He broke out in fresh laughter that made him slump down on the floor and block the doors. A few employees who had been waiting for an elevator seemed to know better than to get involved because they all dispersed and waited on other elevators.

"She's not my girlfriend. And this isn't even close to funny.

She's unconscious and she could have a concussion. It's *your* fault, too."

William pointed to his chest. "Me? I told you to use the panel, not use her head to crack it open." He couldn't even finish the sentence without laughter taking him again. "You know, I'm not sure I can live with myself if I set you two up now. Emily might not survive your next genius plan."

I picked up Emily and started to walk toward the door, but she stirred in my arms. I quickly yanked the fireman's hat off William, snapping the rubber band holding it under his chin in the process. "Say a word of this to her and you're dead."

"What are you going to do, take me under your arm and start ramming through doors with my head? Or maybe you'll try to use me to hammer nails."

I gave him a look that said to be quiet as I eased Emily down to her feet and made sure she could stand.

She blinked her eyes open and put her hand experimentally to her head, which, thankfully, wasn't bleeding. "What happened?"

"We can talk about that later," I said.

"William?" she asked.

"The elevator works again!" he declared as he hopped to his feet and dusted his hands. "It's a Halloween miracle!"

"A Halloween miracle would be if a guy in a mask suddenly stabbed you," I said.

Emily looked a little surprised by my hostility.

"I'm impervious to knives," William said.

"How do you figure that?" I asked.

"Because I've never heard of a rich person stabbing someone. That means the person holding the knife could be bought. Boom. Impervious."

"Want to give me a knife and test your theory?" I leaned closer so only he could hear me. "Butt out. Seriously."

He wiggled his eyebrows. "I'm more of a butt in kind of guy, thank you very much."

"Come on, Emily." I took her hand and pulled her out of the elevator. She followed me up the stairs until we reached the correct floor, and then through a long hallway lined with what looked like conference rooms behind frosted glass windows. At the end of the hallway, the only fully private room waited, and it matched the room number on the key he'd given me.

"This one is yours." I unlocked it and stepped in, but froze in the doorway. The window at the back of the room was covered by a silky red curtain and the only light was provided by two dozen flickering candles. There was a four-poster bed with a mirror on the ceiling above it.

I backed up, forcing Emily away from the door as I did before she had a chance to see inside. I closed it and locked it tight. "Actually," I said. "I think I must have the wrong room."

"What?" she asked. "The key worked though. Right?"

"Just, uh," I tried the door of an empty conference room across the hall and it opened. "Why don't you get set up in here and I'll go let William know you'll be in this room instead. Sound good?"

She looked at me like I was crazy, but smiled. "Sure. I'll get started."

I found William in his office. He was stroking his chin like he fancied himself as some kind of evil genius.

I threw my hands up in the air once I closed the door. "A mirror on the goddamn ceiling? Candles? Four-poster bed? Did I miss any of your genius touches?"

He frowned in thought. "Did you see the flavored massage oils under the bed? Or the quick-start BDSM kit in the closet? Oh, and I had them put in a ridiculous sound system yesterday. You could've rocked half the building with some Barry White if you'd wanted. He's the one people like to fuck to, right? I don't need music, but I've heard that some guys do. I figure you're probably rusty, so—"

"Are you seriously trying to set us up, or are you trying to sabotage any chance of Emily and I ever getting together? Because I'm having a hard time figuring it out."

"I'm hurt that you're even asking me. I want you two lovebirds to bump uglies A.S.A.P.—sorry, that's high up business jargon for 'as soon as possible.'"

"I know what A.S.A.P. means." I clenched my jaw and paced in a circle, wishing I had something I could break to satisfy my frustration. "Did it ever occur to you that I might have a reason for avoiding relationships? That maybe you're not helping me by trying to set me up?"

"No?"

"Well, I don't want a relationship, William. I'm trying really hard to keep things professional with this girl, and you're not helping." The words didn't ring true, even to me, but I was too irritated to care. If I was going to make a mistake by taking things too far with Emily, I wanted it to be my mistake, not his.

He grinned. "So you're saying it *is* working." He twisted in his chair to literally pat himself on the back. "Watch out, Cupid."

"Cupid? Cupid would use his stupid little bow and do something subtle. You're more like Arnold Schwarzenegger with a bazooka."

He nodded in appreciation. "Thank you, man."

"It wasn't a compliment."

"Agree to disagree."

"Look," I snapped. "Emily is taking the conference room next to the one you set up. The one without the bed and the BDSM kit. And nothing is going to happen in there."

He winked. "Got it. The one with the big windows, you dirty dog. If I knew you liked an audience, I wouldn't have had them cover the windows yesterday."

I pointed my finger at him, but couldn't even think of a response that would get through his thick skull. I let my hand drop to my side and left. Trying to change William's mind was pointless. All I could do was be prepared for his next stunt and do my best to avoid it.

9

EMILY

I shoved the last of my supplies into my bag at the retirement home and fought a useless battle against a huge yawn. All the students except Grammy had already filed out. Thankfully, she was wearing her own dentures today.

I'd been teaching them to sculpt pottery, and Grammy's looked suspiciously like a very large penis and balls. She was sitting behind it with a proud look on her face. When I'd confronted her, she claimed it was a butternut squash modeled after her uncle's prize-winning entry when she was just a girl. I didn't believe her or the little twinkle in her eye for a second.

"Is something wrong?" I asked. "You don't usually let Earl get out of here on his own."

"Earl has one foot in the grave." She dismissed the idea of him with a wave of her hand. "I'm more worried about the living, today."

I raised an eyebrow. "You're worried about the living on the night before Halloween? I feel like you have it backwards."

"I haven't seen your little love buddy around here in weeks. I could smell the hormones from the back of the room. I was sure he'd have put a couple babies in you by now."

I shook my head. "It's just a business partnership kind of thing. We get along fine, but I've mainly been working on a project for him. He's throwing a party tomorrow, and I made these posters and some props for the party. Frankenstein statues of clay, some ghosts, you know." It wasn't exactly true. I left out the part where the sexual tension had been thick enough to spread on toast.

"You can spray paint this green and use it for a zombie penis, if you want," she said. She ran a hand down her penis sculpture.

"I thought it was supposed to be your uncle's butternut squash?"

"It is," she said with a wink.

I felt my head reel back a little as I winced. "Uh, well, I'm not sure that's the kind of atmosphere he's going for, but thanks anyway."

Grammy popped out of her chair with all the energy of a twenty-year-old and came to lean on the desk in front of me. "Listen, sweetie. I know my job as the oldest lady in the room is supposed to be saying something prudish. But that's not how I roll, fam."

"Did you just say—"

"Oh yes. I've been on the Instagram. I know all the new slang you kids are using."

I grinned. "Okay..."

"I like to think of myself as a relationship expert. Know why? Because I can recognize when a penis belongs in a vagina. And honey, that man's penis belongs in yours."

"Wow. Okay, I don't know if I'm really comfortable talking about all of this."

"Comfort is for the weak. Do you think anyone ever became a badass by doing what was comfortable? Be a badass, you little whippersnapper. Go get that dick."

She patted me on the cheek and gave me an exact replica of the typical, sweet old lady smile.

I watched her go with a stunned expression. If mental whiplash was a thing, she'd just given me a bad case of it.

A few minutes later, Hailey stuck her head in the door. "Hey, have you seen Grammy?"

I'd met Haily a handful of times, usually at William's side. I'd also seen her cooking show on TV and thought she was adorable. I felt a little starstruck, but nodded. "She was just here. I think her last words were, "go get that dick."

Hailey covered her smile and slipped into the room. She gave me an appraising look. "I don't know if it'd be comforting to say it's not just you, or if that would only make it more weird."

"Something told me it wasn't her first time giving relationship advice."

Hailey sat down at one of the tables and smiled at some memory. "No. Not her first at all. She has a little bit of a fixation on sex. Penises. Vaginas. All the gory details. She loves that stuff. I think she loves it even more because she knows people don't expect to hear her talk about it."

I nodded. "I can see that."

"So who is she trying to set you up with?"

"This guy named Ryan."

Hailey perked up a little at that. "Ryan Pearson?"

I nodded. "I guess I'm not surprised you know him, since he's William's friend."

"Ryan is the one who set William and I up in the first place. Kind of."

"Seriously?"

"Yeah. It's almost ironic that Grammy is trying to set you two up now." She raised an eyebrow and cocked her head. "Almost like fate."

I laughed. "Okay. Stop it with that. I leave the country for art school in January. Fate wouldn't be a big enough jerk to make me fall for some guy right before I have to leave."

"Oh, definitely not. I've heard fate is completely fair and definitely respects your plans."

10

RYAN

Steve was loading up his duffel bag with cleats and all the stuff he needed for practice, and for once, he didn't have a woman over from the night before. It was the day before Halloween, and I'd celebrated with a ridiculously long marathon of horror movies the night before that left me feeling a little bleary-eyed and tired. I'd fought the urge to text Emily and invite her over for another try at date night with a movie marathon. In all my holiday movie watching sprees, I'd never had a problem watching by myself. But last night, I'd spent most of my time distracted and remembering how sweet and soft Emily had smelled, or how her mouth had hung open in an unflattering but adorable way when she fell asleep. She'd even snored a little. She was real, not like some of the women I'd tried and failed to make it work with in the past.

I'd thought about what set her apart instead of paying attention to *Friday the 13th*, and I'd ended up thinking of the perfect test. If you gave a woman a thousand dollars to spend however she wanted, what would she buy first. Without fail, almost every girl I'd dated in the past would've bought clothes, makeup, beer, or maybe even drugs. Emily though? I didn't even know what she'd buy. Probably some stuff for her art, or maybe she'd just take a spontaneous car ride and see a little bit of the world. She might even do something ridiculous like buying a thousand pounds of chocolate. I realized that it didn't matter what she'd do with the money, not specifically. What mattered was that she wasn't like the women before. She didn't fixate on how she looked or buy into the materialism that was so rampant in New York City.

She was real, and so were the feelings I'd felt growing for her since we first met. Instead of my desire to be with her cooling off like I'd expected, it'd been steadily getting more intense until it had started to feel like an out-of-control bonfire.

I'd even ended my horror movie marathon with the last movie Emily and I watched, *The Shining*. It was already one of my all-time favorites before our not-date, and it was one of my most nostalgia-filled experiences. I'd watched it for the first time at a drive-in movie theater. I sat in the back of a van with some of my friends from the neighborhood and had nightmares for weeks. It was perfect.

Steve straightened and tossed his bag over his shoulder. "So?" he asked.

"So what?" I was playing dumb, but I knew exactly what he was asking. I'd been avoiding Emily ever since showing her the workspace at William's office as much as possible. I had a brand new couple that I'd been working to get started on their Bubbly Baker franchise. I didn't know the next move with Emily, so I'd used it as an excuse to bury myself in work, but the party was coming, and it was time for me to check on her. I'd known I couldn't avoid it forever, but I'd hoped some time apart would've helped me feel more level-headed. Instead, I felt like a lovesick puppy that had been apart from my crush for years. This wasn't going to be good.

"That girl who was doing posters for you," Steve said, "I haven't seen her around or heard you talk about her. William said you've been avoiding her *and* him. We had a genius plan drawn up, too. Next time you came to the office, William was going to lock you guys in the stairwell together and we had this intern girl who was going to do a thing kind of like *The Ring*. You know, hair over the face and all that."

I sighed. "I'm trying to decide if I should bother asking why you're helping him."

"I've been helping him because I want to see you get with a girl you like, man. Hell, I want you to be with a girl. Period. You're a good guy and I can tell you're not really satisfied. You just run around all day making deals or whatever *Wolf on Wall Street* shit it is you do, and you come back here drained and dead. Last time I saw you look like you were in a good mood was when that girl came around."

"I appreciate it, but I'm good. Seriously. It's like I told William. I'm not looking for a relationship, and you knuckleheads forcing me into one isn't going to help. It's just going to make things messier."

Steve sighed. "Have you tried listening to your penis?"

I frowned. "What?"

"Your penis. I know all those corny movies say listen to your heart, but I've always listened to my penis. And you know where it leads me? Love, man. It's like a thick, perfectly sculpted, eight-inch, throbbing arrow that points me to love. Every time."

"I think you're confusing love and lust. I've got no problem with lust. My problem is with what happens after the chemicals stop pumping and people have time to learn to hate each other."

"Yeah, well, the first step is your penis. Listen to the thing, let it start you down the right path. You have a little fun, and if it doesn't work out, it doesn't work out. How else are you supposed to find love?"

I shrugged. "I don't know, man. But I'm not buying the theory that I have to stick my cock in a woman to know if I love her. Who even says everybody has to find someone to love? When did that become the end-all-be-all goal in life?"

"What's your alternative? Making the perfect cupcake and jacking off to a picture of a Christmas tree or something?"

I threw a shoe at him, but he casually ducked out of the way. "No," I said. "It'd be nice if I had a chance to decide for myself though, instead of having you and William try to force me and Emily together."

"Was that her name?"

"What? Yes. Emily White, why?"

"Dude." Steve paused with his eyes to the side and his mouth open. He snapped his fingers and pointed. "Dude!"

"What? Do you know her from somewhere or something?"

"Yes. We both do. We went to high school with her. You don't remember? She was artsy back then, too. Your girlfriend smeared a cupcake on some painting she made and it was this big thing. You seriously forgot all that?"

I thought my stomach might fall out of my body. I hadn't forgotten. Not at all. I just didn't connect the dots between the sweet, funny girl from my Home Ec class to the sweet, funny girl from the retirement home. "Hold on," I said. I went to the bookshelf and dug out my yearbook from senior year. I flipped through until I found her picture. *Emily White.* Senior quote: "That wasn't like *High School Musical* at all."

Steve leaned over my shoulder. "She does look different. Kind of."

"I don't know how I didn't see it." My brain was slowly playing catch up. I couldn't decide if it was a significant discovery, or if it changed nothing.

"You probably repressed it. Your girlfriend ruined that girl's senior project for art class. It was really traumatic. For her, at least. I thought the whole thing was kind of hilarious."

I shook my head. "No wonder she has been so adamant about

avoiding a relationship. She probably thinks I've just been pretending I didn't remember her."

"Then go apologize. *Go to her,* man. Say you're a dumbass and you only just realized you knew her before. Wait till it's raining and then pick her up and spin her around a little bit. Then you apologize. Kiss. Fondle. Penetrate."

"You're right about one thing, at least."

"Which thing?" he asked as I grabbed my things and headed for the door. "The penetrate part?"

I COULDN'T WAIT FOR THE ELEVATOR AT GALLEON WITHOUT replaying the ridiculous series of events that followed last time. It had been almost two weeks now. Realizing she was the same girl from high school shouldn't have changed anything. I still didn't do well with relationships. I still had a trail of horrible romantic failures in my past.

And yet, I felt something different. I remembered all the conversations I'd had with her now. Back then, I'd been an idiot, and I had followed along with Steve's theory of dating: the hotter a girl was, the better idea the relationship was. But then the ordinary girl in my Home Ec class had rocked my understanding of women. I'd actually enjoyed talking to her. Gradually, she hadn't looked so ordinary to me, either.

When Haisley found out that I was spending more time than I had to with Emily, she got jealous. I'd just shared a few of the cupcakes Emily and I made for Home Ec that day, and she went storming off in a jealous rage, cupcake in hand. By the time I found her, she had smeared blue icing all over Emily's painting that was on display outside the art room.

Being the idiot that I was, I did the worst thing possible. I took the fall for Haisley, because I thought that was the *honorable* thing to do. I was her boyfriend, after all. Haisley thought the act somehow meant I still had feelings for Emily, and Emily thought

I really did it. And just like that, I ruined my chances with both of them at the same time.

I took a deep breath outside the conference room where Emily had all the artwork set up and displayed for me. It looked like a slice of Halloween heaven inside, with a giant Frankenstein monster, ghosts, a hairy tarantula the size of a German Shepherd, and a stack of the gorgeous posters she'd made. I'd already seen the posters because I had her email pictures of them to me as soon as she was done and let William handle posting them all over Galleon and I'd put them up in my bakeries.

She smiled when she saw me. She was pulling at her fingers and chewing her lip as I looked at everything.

"It's all amazing," I said.

She let out a breath and smiled wider. "I think Frankenstein should've been a little taller, but I misjudged on some measurements."

"He looks perfect to me. Hey, Emily..."

"Oh, nope, nope!" She said, waving her hands like she was trying to hold me back. "I get it. You don't have any more work for me after this. I wasn't expecting this to be some kind of ongoing arrangement. So we can skip the awkward you're technically fired but it's not really like you're fired thing. I already put two and two together when you kind of ghosted me, so—"

I laughed. "That's not what I was going to say, actually. I wanted to tell you that I remember you. Before I came today. You're the Emily from high school. We had Home Ec. I was an ass. I kind of ruined everything? Ringing any bells?"

She twitched her head to the side a little and gave me a crooked smile. "I recognized you. I just didn't want to make it awkward."

"Too late."

"You don't need to explain. Really. It was a long time ago. I get it."

"I do though. I feel kind of like I'm taking the easy out here, but I want you to know I wasn't the one who smeared a cupcake on your painting. I took the fall for Haisley because I was a dumbass and I thought it was the kind of thing I was supposed to do as her boyfriend."

"Seriously, don't worry about it. It's not like I have a voodoo doll of you in my closet that I torture every night out of spite or anything."

"See, I know you're lying because I saw your apartment. There wasn't even room for a closet in there."

She grinned. "Got me." She paused, working her lips to the side in thought. "Didn't you and Haisley break up almost right after the whole cupcake thing?"

"Yeah. I don't know if you know this about me, but every relationship I've ever been in has crashed and burned. I'm pretty sure I have some kind of curse. No matter how well it starts out, every relationship I touch is doomed."

"Is that why you've been able to resist my womanly charms?"

I laughed. "I wouldn't say I've completely resisted them."

"No?" she chewed her lip again, but this time, it sent a small shockwave of heat through me.

"Hey," I said quickly, more to diffuse the heavy air that seemed full of potential than because I had something worth saying.

She waited expectantly, eyebrows high.

"Uh, I wanted to invite you to the party. Tomorrow. I figured you knew you were invited anyway, but I don't actually have a plus one. So I thought maybe you could come with me. As friends, or something."

"Or something? Can I choose the 'or something' option?"

I chuckled. "As friends."

"Okay. I'll come to the party with you, as your friend. Are the rules the same as at the gastropub? We have to make sure we're not having fun or it turns into a date?"

"Definitely. And make sure you don't wear a sexy Halloween

costume, because if there's a massacre at the party, by horror movie rules, the sexier your costume is, the faster you die."

She thought about that for a second. "Wow. I think you're actually right. Horror directors hate the slutty Halloween costume. I guess I'll dust off my Bill of Rights costume."

I squinted at her. "I can't tell if you're making that up or if you're serious."

"I guess you'll just have to wait for tomorrow night to find out. Won't you?"

11

EMILY

I stood in front of my bathroom mirror, which was decorated with water spots because I apparently brushed my teeth like a barbarian. I probably flossed like a maniac, too, but that was only once every six months—right before dentist visits.

I had been joking about the Bill of Rights costume, but one perk of being an artist and having familiarity with a range of fabrics and mediums was that I'd been able to whip a costume together last night and this morning. I was now a full-sized Bill of Rights.

I stared at my reflection and wondered if I'd taken the whole "not slutty" thing a bit to the extreme. I looked like a rolled up newspaper. My legs stuck out the bottom of the costume just above the knees, my arms were attached to matching sleeves so only my hands were free, and my face visible by an oval cutout. I'd made the whole costume from a fabric that was light enough to bend but would still look like paper, and I'd spent several hours painstakingly writing down what I could fit of the bill on my costume.

If I hadn't worked so hard on it, I probably would've backed out. I looked ridiculous, but that was probably for the best, anyway. I was already walking a thin line by agreeing to come to the Halloween party with Ryan in the first place. Trying to dress sexy or hope that he'd like how I looked was putting one foot into some very dangerous territory. When I'd freshly been caught up in him, I was ready to forget all about Paris. The day he took me to Galleon, I probably would've gone along with anything he wanted. But time apart had been good. I'd worked on the art and I'd had a chance to remember why it was so important to me.

I felt whole when I was working with my hands and making something. I was addicted to the challenge of trying to improve, and to the final moment of satisfaction when I saw how my hard work and focus had taken something rough and turned it into a completed project. In a perfect world, I could still pursue that *and* get the guy I wanted, but the world wasn't perfect, and I knew my future in art led through Paris.

Maybe I should've gone dressed as my acceptance letter to art school in Paris just to be sure I kept my thoughts in the right place.

There was a knock at my door.

I opened it up to see Lilith, who was dressed in one of her normal outfits, but it was spattered with blood and there was a perfect, bloody handprint around her shin. She was holding a rolling pin covered in dried blood.

"Nice costume," I said.

"What costume?" she asked. "I just didn't have time to shower after my date."

"You know you're creepy when your best friend isn't a hundred percent sure that was a joke."

"Who said we're best friends?" she asked.

I punched her shoulder. "I did."

She gave me a rare smirk. "Fine. If you're going to be weird about it, we can call it that. And I might kind of like Halloween, okay? But if you tell anyone I was in a good mood, I'll murder you and everybody will just think your corpse is a decoration until tomorrow. I'll be in Mexico before they find out."

"Yeah right," I said, putting my hands on my knees and leaning forward. The top of my costume extended about a foot and a half past my head, which let me swing it at Lilith like I was trying to swat a fly with a newspaper. I swung my hips around and started chasing her out into the hallway until I finally pinned her against the wall with a solid blow.

To my surprise, she was fighting to hold back a smile. "That was the dumbest looking thing I've ever seen," she said.

"I've known the Chamberson brothers a few months," said Ryan, "so I can't say the same."

"Ryan!" I squawked. I straightened too fast and the weight of my costume started pulling me backwards. I pinwheeled my arms for balance, but it was useless. I thudded to the floor, but hardly felt the impact because of all the padding.

Ryan and Lilith stood above me, looking down.

Ryan was dressed in a suit, but he had some kind of baby carrier strapped to his chest with a bag of sugar inside.

"A sugar daddy," I said from the ground. "Nice."

He grinned. "You're the only one who got it so far. I knew I liked you."

"Someone is going to have to help me up."

"Please don't," Lilith said. "I kind of want to watch her flop around and try on her own."

Ryan extended a hand. "I feel like I got my fill from watching her swat you with her giant, oversized head."

I let him pull me to my feet, but frowned. "You just mean the head of my costume, right?"

"Oh, absolutely. Your real head is the perfect size."

"He said you're perfect. And he likes you. Gross," Lilith made a gagging motion. "If you're going to get her pregnant, make sure it's a girl. Little boys are unbearable once they hit middle school age, and I can't promise I wouldn't off the kid as soon as he asks if my phone had any games."

"I'm not even going to respond to that," I said.

"That counts as a response," Lilith said.

"You should've told me you two got along so well," Ryan said to Lilith. "I would've offered to be your personal driver a long time ago."

"You're driving us to the party?" I asked. It was probably a stupid question, but my head was still spinning from using myself as a human flyswatter a few seconds ago.

"That's the plan. At least it was, until I realized I could kidnap you and pull a Nicolas Cage from *National Treasure*. Now I'm kind of tempted just to be able to say I did it."

"Actually." I held up my finger. I knew I was being the stereotypical, obnoxious "um, actually" girl, but I couldn't stop myself. "Nicolas Cage steals the Declaration of Independence in that movie."

Ryan smirked. "Didn't realize you were a fan of the late great Nicolas Cage and his impressive filmography."

"Nicolas Cage died?" Lilith asked.

"He should have," Ryan said.

"That's horrible." I couldn't help laughing. "I happen to like Nicolas Cage, the actor and the person, thank you very much."

"Wait," Ryan said. "Are you serious? What could you possibly like about him, except *Con Air*. I'll admit, I kind of liked that movie."

"He's probably immortal, for one. Does anyone know how old he is? *No.* He's also hilariously bad with his money. He's bought a shark, a genuine collection of shrunken heads, and a private island right next door to Johnny Depp's private island, just to name a few."

Ryan was holding back laughter and Lilith was giving the *I've-heard-this-speech-a-dozen-times-already* look to the ceiling.

"Did he really buy a shark?"

"That's the least believable part to you?"

"It's just the most impractical. I mean, where do you keep it? Aren't you worried it's going to break free and eat you?"

"Sharks can't walk on land, dumbass," Lilith said.

Ryan glared at her. "It'd just need to aim one perfect jump. Free Willy style."

I nodded. "He's right. It'd be a kamikaze move, but it could work."

"God," she rolled her eyes. "You dorks deserve each other. And on second thought, don't even make a girl. Your DNA needs to die off with you."

Ryan shook his head and laughed. "The fact that I'm having this discussion with a giant replica of the Bill of Rights makes me feel like I'm in some kind of weird fever dream."

Lilith swung her rolling pin at Ryan's elbow.

He jumped back and grabbed his arm. "What the Hell?"

"Just wanted to prove you weren't dreaming," she said with a casual shrug.

I'D KNOWN THE WORK I DID FOR RYAN WAS MEANT FOR A PARTY OF over two thousand people, but the sheer scope of the event hadn't clicked until we arrived at Galleon. The lobby was untouched by Halloween decorations, to my surprise, but I hardly noticed with the huge groups of costumed people heading for the elevators. I had a moment of giddy pride when I saw my posters plastered all over the lobby. I'd already seen them several times as I came and went, but the excitement of seeing what was really my first officially commissioned piece of art on display still hadn't faded.

My pride was short-lived, because a quick glance told me that no other women here were worried about dying first in the event of a Hollywood horror showdown. In fact, it looked like they might actually be competing to see who had dressed provocatively enough to be killed first.

I sucked in a breath, straightened my back, and soldiered on. Let them flaunt their boobs. Psh. A real man doesn't care about cleavage, he cares about an inalienable right to bear arms, right? And guess what, that particular right was plastered right across my butt. That's right. I was a dirty girl, and I wasn't going to apologize.

"No decorations down here?" I asked Ryan.

"Bruce wouldn't let it happen. He said it was bad enough having to allow this ridiculous party in his building without us 'tainting' the lobby while we were at it. But the joke's on him, because I put a few fake spiders on the toilet seats down here and William helped me booby trap his office."

Lilith stopped in her tracks. "You guys booby trapped Bruce's office?" She thought about that for a few seconds, and then something like a robot's idea of what a smile was supposed to look like touched her face.

By the time we reached the elevators, Lilith was lost in the shuffle of people, but somehow, Ryan managed to stay close by my side.

"Should we wait for her?" asked Ryan.

"No. She would ditch us before long, anyway." I let the crowd jostle me closer to the elevators while I tried to make a battle plan. I'd accepted Ryan's invite and known he might have only been saying I could come as a courtesy. It was highly likely that he hadn't even planned on making an effort of finding me in the crowd once I arrived. Instead, he'd shown up to give me a ride, and now he was talking like he was planning on sticking together.

The art school half of my brain was flashing warning alarms, but the female side of my brain was twirling a bra on its fingertip while it sipped a sloppy martini.

I started hearing the music as soon as we were in the elevator. We rode it up to the top floor and had to squeeze our way out through a man dressed as a vampire and a woman dressed as a succubus—or maybe she was just dressed as a woman in her underwear with a tail and wings, I couldn't tell the difference.

My breath caught at the sight of the party. The ceiling trailed up at least four or five stories. Huge swinging props were dangling from the ceiling and swaying, including one of the ghosts I'd made. A fog machine clouded the floor and drifted up to the sky, creating little swirls of mist where the ghost broke through. I wanted to clap with delight. It looked so real and spooky. It was like I'd stepped inside one of the inexplicably high-budget Halloween parties from my favorite old-school horror movies. Orange and black lights pulsed in the fog like some kind of creepy thunderstorm waging at our feet, and a live band dressed as zombies played on a stage in the center of the room.

There was too much to take in. There were decorative touches everywhere I looked, from the hollowed out pumpkins holding the punch, to the ramshackle little huts that had been erected and scattered around the party. I could just barely see shrunken heads and all kinds of gross but wonderful props jammed inside them.

"This was all you?" I asked. I had to raise my voice to be heard over the music.

He shrugged. "Sort of. I basically chugged a few energy drinks, stayed up late, and wrote down all the ideas. I gave it to William and told him to use his money to make it happen."

I grinned. "You did a little more than that to get one measly ghost, a Frankenstein, and some posters out of me."

"Well, I think that ghost is clearly the centerpiece of the party. I needed to make sure the artist was capable."

"It was so important that you never checked how it was coming or came to see it until right before the party?"

He sighed. "If you're trying to corner me into admitting you're special and I gave you way more attention than every other part of setting this party up, it'll never happen."

I smiled contentedly. "That was close enough to an admission. I'll take it."

He smiled wryly and grabbed my hand. "Come on, let's see if you can dance in that ridiculous costume."

"Pause!" I said. "I think you're going to have to find some alcohol and put it in me before you get me to dance in this."

"You want me to put it in you?" he asked. There was a glint in those light brown eyes that told me everything I needed to know.

I cleared my throat. "There's a lot of things you need to put in me."

He raised his eyebrows. "If this turns into a play on words about your costume, I'm going to be disappointed."

I laughed. "First, you need to put an apology in my ears for being a dickbag in high school."

"I thought I already did that, but I'll say sorry as many times as you want me to." He leaned forward and then stopped, grinning. "Your ears are kind of behind the weird little sleeve thing around your head, though."

I tugged at my costume until my ear popped out and then tilted it toward him.

His voice was a warm rush of air in my ear. "I'm sorry for being a dickbag in high school."

He stayed dangerously close to me, but pulled back enough that I could see his face. "Now, what do you want me to put in you next? Because if you're all out of ideas, I've got a few."

I wanted to laugh, but the only sound that came out was a choked kind of gurgle. I'd expected some slow flirtation and a lot of trying to read the tea leaves to gauge his interest. This was more like a shotgun to the face. "You know how master chess players are always like, ten moves ahead?"

"What, are you going to say I'm checkmated now or something?"

"No. I'm going to say I was always horrible at chess, and I was hoping some more clever follow-ups would come after the put it in my ear thing." I shrugged and grinned. "That was the best I had."

He smiled in that way guys have been smiling since the stone age—the one where they have that obnoxiously charming twinkle in their eye that says they're reading you like a book, and they're on the part where the sexy music starts playing and the light dims.

I licked my lips. I wanted to take a snapshot of the moment, because I knew it was a crossroad. Two paths forked out in front of me. One was safe. It led to the future I'd been carefully building for years. It led to the thing I'd been dreaming about as long as I could remember. It was the smart choice—the obvious choice.

The other was dangerous. It followed a guy I still didn't really know. It was the impulsive path and the reckless one, where nothing was guaranteed and nothing was set in stone. But when I thought about the path that led to art school, I pictured a plain, boring door. When I thought about the one that led towards Ryan, it felt like I'd be walking into the kind of fantasy life I only saw in movies, where every day was electric with potential.

Maybe there was a third choice. I didn't have to marry myself to one path or the other. I could have fun tonight, and I could stop worrying so much about what might happen in a few months and just focus on tonight.

"Excuse me." A man and a woman walked up to stand beside us. It was Bruce Chamberson and his wife, Natasha. "You were one of the artists who worked on the decorations, right?" he asked.

I'd barely spoken with Bruce, but somehow, seeing him inside his own building made him all the more intimidating. "That depends," I said slowly. "Do you like them?"

He scanned the ceiling and the room with a look between disgusted and confused. "For what they are, sure."

Ryan leaned in to whisper in my ear again. "From him, that's a compliment."

"Thank you. But where's your costume?" I asked him.

He grimaced and looked down at his perfectly normal suit. "You know that commercial with the guy in the suit? The one where he says he's mayhem?"

"You're him?" I asked. "Shouldn't you be... sabotaging things? You know, getting in character?"

"No. I'm not him. I was just wondering if you'd seen the commercials. Always thought those were funny. I don't wear costumes, I think it's childish."

His wife, Natasha, gave me an amused smile. "He's great at parties, isn't he?"

I grinned. "Reminds me of a friend of mine, a little bit."

"What are you, a newspaper?" Natasha asked.

"I'm the Bill of Rights. It's a long story." I took in her costume. She had small pillows taped to almost every inch of her body. "What are you supposed to be?"

"I'm accident prone."

I frowned in thought as I tried to dig out the wordplay, but Ryan's chuckling laughter drew my attention. "What? Am I missing the joke?"

"No," she sighed with a smile. "Like, literally. I'm very accident prone, and Bruce said this was the perfect excuse to dress me in a way where I couldn't hurt myself. What was it you said?" she asked him.

"For one night of the year, I can take you out and know you're not going to crack your head or break an ankle when I take my eyes off you. Everybody will think it's a costume."

"But you've still been watching me like a hawk," she said, then she got on her tiptoes and gave his chin an adorable little kiss.

He cupped hers in his thumb and forefinger and kissed her forehead with an unapologetic shrug. "I'm overprotective."

She smiled at me. "He's just lucky I didn't really have a

costume I was excited to wear. He's also lucky I love naps, and I always wondered how comfy this would be. Lay down anywhere and you're automatically in a bed. It's perfect."

I laughed.

Ryan cleared his throat.

Bruce dug in his jacket and tried to hand Ryan a cough drop.

"I don't have a cough," Ryan said. "When someone clears their throat while making eye contact, it usually means you're doing something wrong, like interrupting a man who was trying to convince a woman to dance."

Bruce looked from Ryan to me, and then nodded seriously. "Just one question, then. Have you seen William? He was supposed to be here by now."

Ryan groaned. "No, I haven't seen him, and I'm not thrilled to hear he's missing."

"That makes two of us," Bruce said.

"Why?" I asked.

Ryan sighed. "When you can't find William, it's usually because he's doing something stupid. I also invited my roommate, Steve, and he's basically William minus the subtlety. The two of them missing at the same time is a recipe for bad."

"You're right about William, at least. He has a history of trying to pull stupid pranks on Halloween, too. Good luck."

"You too."

Bruce and Natasha left, and Ryan turned his attention back to me. He looked around the party and then gave a quick shrug. "You were saying I needed to put something in you. Why don't I start with a little alcohol?"

"I would allow that."

We grabbed drinks and headed upstairs to an area where a balcony with a glass wall overlooked the party below. There were tables and more Halloween decorations set up, as well as some old-fashioned TVs playing classic, black and white horror movies.

"Nice touch," I said, pointing to one of the TVs. "What is this room for, anyway? I don't think it's exactly normal for an office building to have... whatever this is on the top floor."

"It's William's fault. He wouldn't budge until Bruce agreed to plug a party venue in at the top of the building. He claimed it would be for schmoozing new clients and that sort of thing. I have no idea if they actually do that, but it does make for a good holiday party spot."

"Rich people," I said slowly as I looked around the room and tried to imagine having so much money that you could afford something like this in New York if you didn't use it all the time.

He nodded and gave a distracted smile as we took a seat near the corner. The music wasn't as loud up here, and I didn't have to raise my voice to be heard anymore.

"Something wrong?" I asked.

He shook his head, but then shrugged. "I mean, not *wrong*. No. But every time I've had anything close to feelings for a girl, it only takes two or three days for all the romantic ideas to fade away."

"Wow," I said with a half-smile. "It's a good thing I never came close to falling for you, or that would be a little disappointing."

He licked his lips and his eyes met mine. Even from across the table, I could almost feel a spark of energy pass between us. "Right. It's a good thing you never had feelings for me. Because then I *really* wouldn't know what to do."

"You're going to have to elaborate," I said. "I know women are supposed to be good at reading between the lines on this kind of stuff, but I've always been horrible at it. Also, I feel really weird having a serious conversation like this while I'm dressed as The Bill of Rights. I just thought that was worth noting."

He hardly seemed to hear me. The look on his face was deadly serious, and seeing him look at me that way made my mouth feel dry and my stomach feel fuzzy and warm.

"It has been a lot more than two or three days, Emily. None of my feelings are fading away. They're only getting stronger. I tried not to lead you on because I was so sure it'd happen, and now... Now I'm just sitting here wondering why I've waited so long to take what I want."

I bit my lip. His gaze was magnetic. It sucked me in and refused to let me look away.

I couldn't think. I could hardly breathe. Paris seemed distant and silly and unimportant in that moment. Deep down, I knew I'd regret it later. I knew Paris and my future would come rising back up. I knew all of that, but I couldn't stop my pounding heart from doing the thinking and the talking.

"Well," I breathed. "Whoever this girl is. You'd better go to her, then. It sounds serious."

The corner of his mouth inched upward in a hypnotizingly slow way until he was showing just the faintest glimmer of a smirk. "You're right."

He stood up, pushed his chair in, and waved to me as he started walking away from the table and back down toward the party.

I frowned and sat up straight. *Wait, what?* I stood from my chair and involuntarily took a step toward him. Before I had time to have a mental meltdown, he turned around and his smirk widened into a grin as he walked back toward me and reached for my hand.

"Sorry," he said. "I couldn't resist."

"What? Giving me a heart attack?" I let him take my hand in his, and there was no mistaking the way his fingers felt against mine. It was soft, perfect, and full of intention. The music thudded from downstairs, sending small shockwaves through my chest. My head felt light, almost weightless. The only thought my brain seemed to have room for was to wish with all of my being that I was wearing anything other than a ridiculous Bill of Rights costume that didn't make me look like a giant, rolled up news-paper with a face.

"I warned you that every relationship I've ever been in has failed, right?"

I tried to keep a straight face as I answered. "Who says I'm willing to be in a relationship with you? We're just holding hands."

"Yeah, but we're not even using protection."

I laughed. "Wow. You're right. I think I can already feel the missed period coming. This is more serious than I thought."

He slid his hand around the back of my costume and gave a slight squeeze as he raised an eyebrow. "I think I just fondled your rights, too. So, yeah, you could say it's getting very serious."

I bit back a smile. I'd never felt this kind of energy before. There was an unstoppable gravity pulling us together, and now that I noticed it, I realized it'd been there from the beginning.

"Bad news," William interrupted.

Ryan stepped to the side and turned to see William, who was standing a few feet from us with a worried expression on his face. He was dressed plainly, to my surprise.

"William," Ryan said tightly. "You're kind of interrupting something."

William gave him a look like he was crazy, then he grinned at the sugar in Ryan's baby carrier. "Sugar daddy? Nice. And Emily is... *Yikes.*" He cringed. "Competing for the least sexy costume award?"

I put my hands on my hips, which probably didn't have the same effect when I was dressed like this.

"Don't get me wrong," he said quickly. "You uh, wear that well, even if you do look a little bit like a dick in a condom." He burst out in uncontrollable laughter at his own joke.

Ryan watched him impatiently. "She's the Bill of Rights, dumbass. And at least she wore a costume."

William turned to show us his back, which was covered in nickels that had apparently been glued to his suit.

"Nickelback?" Ryan groaned.

"Ding ding. Now come on, I need you two on the roof. It's a surprise."

"I'm actually pretty happy right here," I said.

William waved me off. "Nobody asked the history nerd."

"Careful," Ryan warned.

"Ohh, what's this?" William asked. "I think I'm starting to smell a little something and it smells a lot like love."

Ryan looked like he was a few syllables away from giving William a black eye. "If I go to the roof with you, can I push you off?"

"So much violence. But yes, you're welcome to try. I doubt you'll want to when you see the wonderful little surprise I whipped up, though. Come on."

"Are we really going up to the roof with him?" I asked.

Ryan sighed. "William is like a dog. You can give him a scrap of food and he'll stop begging, or you can try to ignore him and he'll ruin your meal."

"I can hear you, but you're also not wrong. I had a plan 'B' if you tried to ignore me, and it wasn't going to be nearly as pleasant."

We followed William, and the whole time, I was replaying those last few moments with Ryan. I'd felt something there. In his touch. In his eyes. Everywhere. I'd let it soak into me and instead of feeling scary or wrong, it just felt right.

Ever since I'd seen him again for the first time in so many years, I'd been trying to stop myself from listening to my feelings. I finally thought I was ready to open up to them and let this happen.

Of course, that would all be easier if William Chamberson didn't have the world's worst timing.

Hailey stopped us just before the elevators. She was dressed as a peanut butter jar, and honestly might have had me beat for the least sexy costume at the party. She had what looked like an almost perfect replica of a giant plastic jar of peanut butter encasing her body, except where her face stuck out of a narrow little window and her arms and legs poked through.

"Wow," I said.

"Wow to you, too." She pointed to my costume. "That's pretty awesome. The Bill of Rights? Is that a play on words, or is it just kind of like... 'Hey, I'm the Bill of Rights?'"

"It's what happens when I get so caught up in wondering if I can do something that I forget to stop and ask if I should. What about yours?"

Hailey glared at William, and I saw the most adorable mixture of love and irritation in her eyes, like she wanted to be upset with him but she couldn't, because whatever he'd done was so perfectly him. "It was supposed to be a team costume. I'd be peanut butter and he was going to be a basketball player."

"Peanut Butter jam?" I asked. "Nice."

"It would have been," Hailey said. "But somebody said they kept getting wedgies from their basketball shorts and bailed on me at the last minute."

William crossed his arms and tried to look indignant. "No man should have to endure that much fabric going up his ass crack. I'm sorry. Ask The Bill of Rights," he said, nodding toward me. "I bet there's something in there about that. The founding fathers would've mentioned some sort of inalienable right to freedom from wedgies."

Hailey gave me a look that said, 'pray for me.' She reached for William's hand. "Come on. I bribed the DJ to play peanut butter jelly time when I give the signal. I need you to be there to dance backup for me."

William dipped his chin and growled appreciatively. "I knew we were soulmates. I bribed the DJ to play Nickelback. I was just going to stand at the front of the crowd and point to my back. A gentleman would let you go first, but..."

She rolled her eyes and grinned. "You can go first. I can see you're excited."

William seemed to remember we were standing there, and he suddenly gave us a little shove toward the staircase. "Use the stairs to get the roof. It's part of the surprise. Go, go. I've got a wife to seduce, and you'd better get out of here so I don't accidentally seduce the two of you, too."

"Why do I feel like we're walking into some kind of trap?" I asked him.

"Because we almost definitely are."

"Okay, have fun. Make lots of babies. I call dibs on naming the first one! Good luck!" William slammed the door behind us, and my heart sank when I heard the lock click.

"He just locked it," I said.

Ryan checked the door and sighed. "Yeah."

"Why don't you seem surprised?"

"I'm going to be totally honest here." Ryan looked uncharacteristically nervous, and somehow, it was a mouthwateringly sexy combination. "William and Steve have been trying to set us up since the get-go. You know the whole robbery thing?"

I felt my stomach sinking as my brain started connecting the dots. "Yes…"

"The two 'robbers' were William and Steve. I didn't find out until you left to make the call."

"But you let me keep thinking it was a robbery. Do you have any idea how many self-defense videos I've watched on YouTube since then? I even made an anonymous post in an online forum talking about my experience, for God's sake!" I was somewhere between pissed off, confused, and oddly enough, relieved. "I could probably fight my way off a pirate boat by now."

"That kind of sounds like a good thing?" he said slowly.

I jabbed my finger at him. The normal self-consciousness I felt was being overwhelmed by a mixture of embarrassment and anger. "Don't try to turn this into a good thing. I don't get it. Why wouldn't you just tell me?"

"At the risk of sounding pathetic, I was worried you would think I put him up to it if I told you. And then I thought I'd find a better time, but I was probably just kidding myself because I was worried you'd want nothing to do with me if you found out."

"The elevator. That's why you were acting so pissed at him, and why you responded to the firefighter on the intercom the way you did."

He nodded, but said nothing more. He didn't try to deafen me with excuses or change the subject. It looked like he was just willing to wait and accept whatever my feelings were on the matter. Easier said than done, considering I didn't even know how to feel.

"So why keep going along with his scheme just now?" I rattled the doorknob a little more angrily than I planned.

"Well, for the first time, I didn't think I'd mind it if William tried to force us together."

I closed my eyes. Even though part of me wanted to reach out and hug him because I knew what he was saying was sweet, he'd still betrayed my trust. I started tearing off my costume, because on top of already feeling like I was the village idiot for not seeing what was happening, I *looked* like an idiot.

"What are you doing?" he asked.

"Getting out of this stupid, freaking, costume—*urgh*!" I lost my footing when pulling my legs up and out of the suit and rolled down the stairs. My world spun, and by some miracle, my face never caught one of the steps, and I was sent bumping and bouncing down until I thudded into the wall at the bottom. My knees and elbows stung a little, but I thankfully didn't seem to be hurt.

Ryan rushed down and skidded to his knees beside me. He ran his hands over my arms and legs, eyes intent on finding any injuries.

"I'm fine," I said, shaking him off and getting to my feet. I finished stripping out of my costume, which unfortunately left me in a skin-tight, beige-colored bodysuit that probably was almost as ridiculous as my costume itself. I slammed the costume to the ground and jabbed my finger at him. "And don't even think about laughing!" I said.

He held up his hands like my finger was a gun and shook his head, but I could've sworn I saw him trying to hold back laughter.

I stormed up the stairs. Maybe some doors below us were unlocked, and maybe I could even get to the lobby and escape from all of this, but I just wanted fresh air, and I knew the roof access had to be close. I started to feel how I'd overreacted and wished I'd taken a few more seconds to think, but pride and anger kept me from going back down and saying so. I had a right to be upset with him, but I could unfortunately see his side, too. William had put him in a crappy position, and he'd made the wrong choice, but it wasn't some malicious act. Forgiveness wasn't just an act of logic, though, and right now, my emotions were still broiling.

I pushed open the roof access door and wasn't sure if I should laugh or cry. Apparently, William planned to strand us together on the roof and force us into some kind of romantic evening.

The roof was decorated with string lights, candles, and flowers. Despite the size of the building, the only part of the roof that seemed accessible was just a little larger than two rooms side by side. The effect was a cozy, dream-like little slice of fantasy on top of New York City.

I jumped back in surprise when I saw Grammy standing by the table with a harmonica in her hand.

"Oh," she said. "There were supposed to be two of you."

"Uhh," I took half a step back toward the door.

"Ryan paid me two hundred bucks to come up here and play some music for you two. I didn't bother telling him I only play the harmonica." She cackled and gave me a wink.

"Wait, Ryan paid you? He made it sound like William set all this up."

"This was Ryan, honey. That boy really wants to get in your pants, in my expert opinion. When a man gets out the candles, it's pretty much a flashing neon sign. They think if they make an effort, the least we can do is unzip and say thank you the way God intended."

I felt my anger faltering against Grammy's ridiculousness. "I never saw anything about that in the Bible."

"Be fruitful and prosper. Something like that. Fruits are babies. You know how babies are made?" She held up one finger in the shape of a circle and pressed her index through it with raised eyebrows. "Beautiful, sweet, lovemaking. That's how. Let thine uglies bump upon the ugly of the hot guy I plugged in... *well, shit,* I don't remember the exact verse. But it was something like that."

"I don't think there's going to be any of that tonight," I said.

"Speak for yourself. I've got a date after this gig."

I opened my mouth, cringed a little, and then tried to do a manual shut-down on my imagination. "I meant between Ryan and I. We had a fight, I guess?"

"Well, good. Fights mean make up sex. Nobody has to formally apologize. You just get naked, do the deed, and then it's implied that you're both sorry, or else the sex wouldn't have been so good."

I laughed. "Is that also how God intended apologies?"

"No. That's the way *I* intended them." She raised her harmonica to her lips and belted out an ear-piercingly bad string of sounds, then gave me a wiggle of her eyebrows. "Now you let that boy apologize to you. Also, I ate all the shrimp because I got hungry. But there's some crackers and wine on the table."

She walked past me to the door and slapped my butt. "Cute little suit. What are you, a sperm?"

She closed the door behind her before I even had time to form a response.

I moved toward the table and saw the discarded tails of about three dozen shrimp. The woman had a serious appetite, apparently. I didn't get a chance to straighten out my thoughts before the door to the roof opened again.

12

RYAN

Grammy had refused to explain why she was leaving early, or agreed to give me back my two hundred dollars when I passed her on the way up the stairs. I'd gone down a few flights of stairs and tried the doors, just to see if we were truly locked into this idiotic plan of mine. The apology hadn't gone exactly as I'd imagined, and I thought maybe I could calm Emily down if I just took her back inside. Unfortunately, William seemed to have locked all the doors below us, too. For once in his life, the man had decided to be an overachiever, and he'd screwed me in the process.

I paused before the door to the roof and leaned my head against the metal. It had been so long since I'd felt anything close to this for a woman. Pushing down my feelings for Emily this long only seemed to make them bob back to the surface with even more intensity now that I'd let them out. In the back of my mind, I was still worried that I'd find a way to mess this up, too, but I didn't want to stop. I still wanted this to work.

I could've strangled William. If he had just let things be, Emily wouldn't have been pissed with me. Then again, I couldn't put all the blame on him. If I hadn't been a coward, I could've told Emily right away.

I opened the door and saw her standing by the table. She was still wearing the skin-tight suit of beige material she'd been wearing under her costume, and whether she realized it or not, she looked jaw-droppingly sexy. Every inch of her body was proudly on display, and I was having trouble thinking straight as I took it all in.

"There was supposed to be musical accompaniment," I said, "But she had a hot date, apparently."

Emily turned toward me. The city blazed with light behind her, and she looked like she'd been plucked straight out of a dream. "Your musician said I should let you apologize."

"That was part of the plan here." I gestured to the table, the lights, and the half-eaten food. "Apparently my musician wanted to make my job harder, though."

"Well she helped me calm down, at least." Emily looked thoughtful, then she gave me the faintest smile. "Actually, maybe it would be good for you to have to apologize. I let you off the hook for the cupcake incident in high school, and I was *about* to be too nice and say I forgave you for lying to me pretty much since the moment we met. But no, I want my apology."

I nodded. "And you deserve it, because you deserve better than I've given you. You also deserve a guy who has the balls to come clean with you, even if he's not sure you'll stick around after the fact."

She gestured for me to go on while still wearing that shadow of a smile on her lips.

"And you were the cutest, sexiest Bill of Rights I've ever seen."

She cocked an eyebrow. "You're getting warmer."

"You make an even sexier sperm."

"Colder."

I took a step closer and she took a step back. I kept advancing until she bumped gently against the table, nearly knocking over the glasses of wine. "I've spent most of my adult life avoiding women and relationships because I was so sure they'd fail. I didn't think it was worth the risk anymore. Or the time."

"Colder?" she whispered.

"Ever since I met you, I've been trying to buy my own lie—that it wouldn't work because it never has before, and that I was only setting myself up for failure. But I'm done lying, to you and to myself. You're worth the risk."

"Don't you think it'd be a better apology if you said I wasn't a risk at all?"

I grinned. Her tone was softening, and I could tell I was at least making a little progress. "You did say you were leaving for Paris in a few months. There's always the risk that I won't be willing to let you go, or that you won't want to stay."

"That thought has crossed my mind."

"So what if I promise to let you decide when the time comes. No pressure. No convincing. Worst-case scenario, I get an amazing few months with you and we get to spend the holidays together, and then if you want to go, you go."

"My worst-case scenario is that I don't want to go. I let my dream die because I fall for a guy, and maybe three years from now we break up and I realize I made a huge mistake."

I moved closer until I could feel the heat of her breath on my neck and the soft press of her body against me. "It sounds like we're a match made in heaven. All my relationships fall apart, and you don't want it to last."

She bit back a smile. "So we kiss like the room isn't burning down around us?"

"Exactly." I cupped her chin and tilted her head up and took her lips in mine. She was soft. Warm. Absolutely delicious, and better than I'd ever imagined.

Hunger overcame me in a raw, blood-boiling instant. Adrenaline flooded through me and my head pulsed. All the suppressed feelings and urges of two weeks felt like two lifetimes as my hands roamed her like two starving animals with minds of their own. I cupped her ass and pushed her into me, but the bag of sugar in my baby carrier created a wedge between us.

Emily slid her hands around my back and gripped my baby carrier. "Would it be a turn on if I could undo this with one hand?" she asked.

"Absolutely."

She wiggled her eyebrows and started fumbling with the straps. Her look of confidence slowly faded into frustration and then despair. After a minute of failed attempts, she put her other hand around my back and I heard a click and felt carrier slide off my shoulders. The bag of sugar thumped to my feet, where I scooted it away.

"I loosened it with one hand," she said. She deepened her voice, "Are you not aroused?"

I choked out a laugh. "Was that a Maximus from *Gladiator* reference?"

"Okay, now *I'm* the one who's aroused."

"You mean you weren't already?" I studied her face and ran my thumb over her already swollen and red lower lip. "I thought I was doing okay."

"Hm, I'm not sure. I think I'll need a few more samples before I make an official decision."

I moved closer and felt my erection press into her stomach. She sucked in a surprised breath and locked eyes with me as her lips parted. "That feels more like a five-course meal than a sample."

"Actually, you're not supposed to eat it."

She worked her lips to the side and scowled at me with amusement in her eyes. "I was just thinking about a taste."

"Maybe if you play your cards right."

I took her lips in mine again. I felt she still had words

lingering there, but I couldn't look at them another second without having more. I teased her tongue with mine as I lifted her up to sit her on the table. Plates and dishes clattered to the floor and broke.

"I promise, it's not that my ass is big. This is just a small table," she said.

"Can't it be both?" I asked.

"Only if it's the good kind of big."

"I don't know if you know this about asses, but there's only one kind of big. And it's good."

She grinned. "Correct answer."

"Do I get a prize?"

"Like what?"

"How about a few inches of that zipper on the back of your little body suit down?"

She looked up at me through her thick eyelashes, hesitating.

"I don't know if you remember this, but we're kind of on a deadline here. I don't have the luxury of taking my time with you."

"A few inches," she said carefully.

I took the zipper at the back of her neck and started to pull it down. My eyes locked on the front of her body suit where the fabric began to release its grip on her chest and fall down. Her breasts caught it, giving me a tantalizing, but sadly PG-13 glimpse of her cleavage.

I stood between her open legs, painfully aware of how close I was to having every bit of her in every way that I wanted. I still wasn't wanting to rush it, even if I was teasing her about it.

"And what do I need to do for my next prize?"

"Hmm," she said, licking her lips slowly. "First, you need to get on your knees."

I raised my eyebrows. *Wasn't expecting that.* I did a quick check for any broken glass beneath me, then knelt down. "Okay..." I said, having to tilt my head up slightly to see her now.

"And apologize." She said the words like a demand straight from the mouth of a queen. If it weren't from the faintly mischievous look on her face, I'd almost have believed she was completely serious.

"I'm sorry I cupcaked your art in high school." I kissed the inside of her thigh through her body suit, letting my hands wrap around her legs and force them open a little wider. "I'm sorry I didn't tell you William was staging stupid stunts to try to set us up." I kissed my way a little higher. "I'm sorry I was dumb enough to think I *didn't* want him to succeed at first." I paused just between her legs so that my breath was warm against her. "And most of all, I'm sorry you didn't let me unzip you all the way, because this would've felt a lot better if you had."

Her surprised laughter cut short when I pressed my mouth against her and kissed the fabric between her legs. I could feel the heat radiating there, and I could even taste the faint hint of her sweetness already starting to make its way through her clothes. I explored with the tip of my tongue, feeling through vague hints of shapes beneath the clothing until I was sure I'd found her clit, where I circled for no more than two seconds before she grabbed me by the hair and pulled my head back.

"Okay. You win. All the prizes. Just unzip me and keep doing that."

I pulled her to her feet, knocking more silverware from the table. I reached around and pulled the zipper down, peeling away her clothes like she was a piece of candy, and she might as well have been. I unwrapped her and helped her step out of the last of her costume before tossing it aside. Unfortunately, I threw it a little too hard. The breeze caught it and carried it over the edge of the roof.

Emily looked after it with a stunned expression.

I dragged my eyes across her body, taking in the lacy underwear she was wearing beneath. "I can get back on my knees to apologize for that, too, if you want."

"Down," she said, pushing my head down as she shimmied out of her panties.

She hopped back up on the table and let me press her legs apart. I took in the sight of her with a hungry smile. "Damn, is it too late to take back the part where I said I'd let you leave, no strings attached?"

"Yes, it's too late," she said. "Weren't you supposed to be apologizing?"

I moved closer until her scent enveloped me. She smelled so fucking good. I traced a path up her folds with my tongue and then kissed her clit softly. I didn't move my lips away to speak so that the vibrations and movement would send chills through her. "I'm sorry I threw your sperm suit off the building. And I'm sorry you look so damn good in your underwear that I'm not actually sorry."

She laughed, but the sound was breathless and stilted as she arched her back and pressed herself into me. "Shitty apology."

I sucked her into my mouth and swirled my tongue around her swollen bud, then kissed her deeply, letting my tongue explore every inch of her as I did. I paused just long enough to tease her. "I'm sorry my apologies suck." I emphasized my horrible pun by taking her clit into my mouth again and sucking it against the base of my tongue.

Her entire body shuddered against me, and I was apparently doing a good enough job that she was too distracted to keep giving me a hard time about the quality of my apologies. Thankfully, I was also too distracted to think about how much I was already regretting the deal I'd had to make to get into this situation. It had all sounded easy enough to say, but was I really going to be able to let a girl like this walk away in just a few months?

13

EMILY

Ryan was a magician with his mouth. I'd never exactly been in the hands of a man who came close to what I'd call a sexual expert, and I could tell Ryan was in an entirely different league in seconds. It wasn't just his physical talents or how mouth-wateringly good he looked—even though he was still fully clothed somehow while I was almost totally naked. It was the connection that didn't seem to stop sparking between us like a live, electrical current. Little more than a glance from him set my heart fluttering and my skin tingling with warm butterflies.

So when he finally put his mouth on me, it was an explosion. Maybe it was just trying to resist my natural urges to let something develop with him, or maybe it was all the times we flirted around the idea of it, but one way or another, he was amazing, and I was having a very hard time thinking I'd be ready to leave him behind in January.

I pushed that from my brain. I didn't need to spoil this by thinking about the future, or thinking about *anything* for that matter.

I leaned my head back and let another moan slip out against my will. He was doing things to me with his tongue that I didn't know a man could do. He swirled it *inside* me, sliding along my walls with the most wonderful kind of slick, warm friction I could've imagined. He kissed me there, hungrily even, like I was the most delicious thing he'd ever put his lips to. He blasted away any semblance of self-consciousness I might've had at being naked in front of him with how much he was obviously enjoying himself. Somehow, I thought he was enjoying going down on me as much as I was enjoying it.

I was able to lean back and enjoy myself with no sense of being rushed and no hint that he was just waiting for me to give him permission to stop. It was pure ecstasy. Before long, I was quivering against him, thighs scissoring his head as he licked and kissed me to my first climax.

"I don't think it's supposed to feel that good," I breathed through the aftershocks of my orgasm.

He stood and kissed me while the taste of me was still on his lips. It was dirty, and any other time, I might've thought it was gross, but he made it feel like the sexiest thing in the world. I felt my core clenching all over again and my stomach rage with heat.

"Do I get to make you earn every piece of clothing I take off?" he asked. "Or maybe a few apologies?"

"As far as you're concerned, I'm as innocent as a baby in all of this. You're the bad boy."

"Oh, is that how we're spinning it? You're naked as a baby, at least if it weren't for this bra." He stepped closer and tried to reach around my back for the straps. I leaned back, which had the unintended but not unpleasant effect of making him lean over me more as I knocked what had to be the last plate from the table.

"You want the bra, you've got to offer me a fair trade. A thread for a thread."

He stripped off his tie and flung it to the side. Somehow, he seemed much more able to keep his own clothes from flying over the roof. I grinned as an idea occurred to me. "Actually, I know how you can earn this bra. You need to throw your suit and pants over the roof. I'm feeling generous, so you can keep the underwear, I guess."

"Wow, that's you being generous?"

I crossed my legs and accidentally grazed his erection in the process. I tried to keep a straight face so I could pretend it was part of my seduction routine. "Just for questioning me, your punishment is worse, now. You can keep the suit, because *I'll* be wearing it when we're done here. You get to wear my Bill of Rights costume back to the party."

"You wouldn't," he said.

I almost burst out laughing because he looked genuinely terrified.

"Oh, but I would. I want to see how that cute butt of yours looks behind the right to bear arms."

"Can I express my right to bear ass instead of having to wear that thing?"

I laughed. "No. Until January, that ass is mine, now. And I don't want to share it with any of the women at the party."

"You seem to be under the impression that I'll be done with you before the party ends."

"You're not getting out of this. You put those clothes on the ground. When we go back, you're wearing my costume."

"If I fit in it, that is."

"The material is stretchy."

He sighed. "You're lucky I want nothing more than to fuck you right now."

"You're saying I should make more demands?"

"I'm saying you should shut up and let me have you."

I felt a smile play across my lips. "Well, when you put it like that..."

He stripped out of his clothes, giving me the show of a lifetime. His lean, powerful body towered over me, blotting out the skyline and city lights behind him. When he pulled his undershirt over his head, my breath caught. He bulged in all the right places and had hard, muscular cuts exactly where they should be. My hands physically ached with the need to run across those smooth, warm planes of muscle.

"Pants," I said. I was so beyond caring about looking like the perfect little good girl that I didn't even care what he thought of my horniness. *Yes.* I was horny. It'd been a couple years since I'd been with a guy, and I was on a rooftop in New York City, spread out and almost completely naked on a table in front of a guy who looked like he could've charmed his way into a bank vault. Worse, he was my high school crush, at least up until the cupcake incident.

He paused with his hands on his belt, probably completely aware of how the pose accentuated the sculpted peaks and valleys of his abs and made his forearms bulge. "Hmm," he said slowly. "I think you owe me a bra."

I reached for the strap without taking my eyes off him, but he stepped forward, reaching to stop my hands. "You think I'm going to let you have the fun?"

"No," was all I could manage. My sassy belligerence was starting to fade as desperation roared to life in the depths of my stomach.

"Would it be sexy if I could do it with one hand?" he asked.

I gave him a sour look, but he made what felt like a single, quick motion with his fingers and my bra fell to my lap. I clapped my hands to my breasts in surprise a second later and laughed. "Wow. Why are you so good at that?"

He wiggled his fingers. "Talented fingers." He carefully peeled my hands away from my breasts and looked down at them admiringly.

I'd never been genetically gifted in the chest department, and it took all my willpower not to clap my hands back over myself. All I could think was how his memory must be filled with girls who looked like supermodels and their perfect, perky breasts, and how sad mine must be in comparison.

If he was thinking anything like that, he didn't let it show. He bent down to bring his mouth to my nipple and very slowly took it between his lips and swirled his tongue there.

I arched my back and gasped. More than the sensation, I was flooded by a kind of relief and acceptance. Without a word, he made me feel perfect. Complete. *Beautiful.*

I threaded my fingers through his hair and held him to me as he kissed every inch of my bare skin, wrapping me in his heat and his passion. "Are we really going to be able to stop?" I asked.

"I have a condom. We don't have to." His breath buffeted my chest with every syllable.

"No. I mean when it's time for me to go. Are we making a mistake here?"

"Right now, all I know is my biggest regret in life will be if I have to remember tonight as the night I didn't get to have you."

I pulled him closer to me and let him kiss me as my eyes searched the sky. The lights of the city blotted out the stars, even this late at night, so my view was a hazy yellow blackness. Trying to see through my pleasure to any form of sense was as useless as trying to see the stars, so I closed my eyes and let go of my last thread of resistance.

I reached down to fumble with his belt until he put me out of my misery and did it himself. He kicked off his pants and then his underwear. I tried to steal a peek at the full view, but he was already pulling me toward him to the edge of the table before I had a chance. He slipped a condom on as easily and quickly as he'd undone my bra, then reached down to grip himself and slid inside me.

I gasped. I'd expected a little more of his slow way of making me feel like I had to beg for every inch, but somehow, his sudden-ness felt exactly right. I locked my ankles behind his back, heels digging into the hard muscle there. He planted an arm on the table and his other hand on my thigh and started to slowly work in inch after inch of his length.

I couldn't help letting little whimpering moans spill out of me. My eyes were squeezed shut and I saw white bursts of light against the backs of my eyelids as he made love to me. He didn't just grip me and brainlessly pump away, he *explored* me. I could feel him actively learning me, moan by moan and inch by inch. He was testing and teasing out all of my desires and then putting his new-found-knowledge to work.

The result was like nothing I'd ever dreamed of. He slightly changed the angle of his hips and I could immediately feel a wonderful, body-melting friction against my walls that had me shaking all over. He teased my breasts with his powerful hands and he kissed my jaw, my neck, and all the little, forgotten places in between. Distantly, I felt bad because all I could do was lay back and let him work, like the student before a master. At the same time, I knew it was ridiculous to feel bad. Every single movement of his body telegraphed his absolute pleasure--his unquenchable need to tease out my secret wishes and fulfill every last one.

When my climax finally came, I pressed my mouth against his shoulder to stifle the sound. All the physical and emotional tension that had been building in the background since we'd met came bursting free in a single, fantastic rush. My toes curled and my fingers dug into his back. He tensed, too, making a noise between a grunt and a growl as he pulsed inside me.

My eyes finally opened wide and I took in the sky above me and what I could see of his heaving, broad shoulders as he lay on top of me, still buried deep. With any other man, this was the part where regret, shame, and guilt would start to seep into my thoughts like poison. I searched for them--for any trace--but all I could find was contentment.

14

RYAN

By the time we made it back down to the party through the now-miraculously unlocked stairwell doors, I was wearing a much-too-tight Bill of Rights costume and Emily was wearing my much-too-big suit. Her hair was wild from what we'd just done, and her lips looked swollen and pink.

She slapped my ass through the costume and squeezed hard. "I knew you'd look good in this."

I laughed. "Well, I know I'll be the last one to get stabbed if this turns into a Halloween massacre, at least."

"Is it even Halloween anymore? What is it, two in the morning? Three?"

I looked around the empty building where less than a tenth of the original crowd still lingered. It was in the deep stages of the aftermath of the party. People lounged in corners, clearly far too deep into their drinking. Some still danced, but it was to music over the loudspeakers now instead of from the live band. Others simply sat and talked.

It felt more personal and far less crazy.

I dragged Emily by the hand through the fog and past the witches huts I'd had set up. I found us a relatively quiet spot and gave the universal signal for "want to dance?" I tucked my arm behind my back and extended a hand, which I'm sure had a much less compelling effect when I was wearing her goofy costume. Still, she smiled and took my hand, letting me pull her in close.

"This isn't exactly romantic, slow dance music," Emily said.

"Well, well, well." Steve emerged from the hut beside us and dusted straw off bare chest. He was wearing a leopard print kind of underwear. The girl who emerged behind him wore the same print on her scantily-clad frame. "Do I detect a costume swap?"

"What happened to Jenna?" Emily asked.

The girl behind him crossed her arms and glared. "Yeah, Steve. What happened to Jenna?"

He gave her an easy smile. "My sister is fine, thanks for asking. Come on, Tarzette. We need to leave these two lovebirds to keep awkwardly staring at each other. It looks intense."

Steve dragged the girl away before Emily had a chance to call him on his lie, if she was even planning to.

"Tarzette?" she asked me. "Does he really think—"

"Probably."

Emily clapped her hands to her mouth. "Oh crap." She said. "Weren't you Lilith's ride?"

I cringed. "I mean, she could've called a taxi if she was really ready to go, right?"

"Lilith doesn't do taxis."

"Do I even want to know why?"

"Probably not. But we need to find her. She is not pleasant to be around when she's in a bad mood."

I gave Emily a skeptical look. "If you're trying to convince me that the version of Lilith we normally see is her in a good mood, I'm not buying it."

We eventually found Lilith glaring at a computer screen in an office to the side of the room where the party was held. The door should've been locked, but the broken window said Lilith didn't really care about that minor detail.

"Uh," I said as we stepped through. "This was your handi-work, I guess?"

"Uh, no," she said dryly. She didn't look up from the screen at either of us. "It was like that when I got here. No idea what happened. Must've just been a big gust of wind that blew my shoe right through the thing."

"Lilith," Emily said calmly. She was walking toward Lilith over the crunching glass at her feet like Lilith was a wild animal. "We got locked in the stairwell, or we would've come back to the party sooner. Please don't be mad."

"You got locked in the stairwell and thought maybe her vagina was the lock and your penis was the key, and it took you a few hours to figure out that wasn't working?"

"We didn't sleep together," Emily said.

"I'm sure there was no sleeping. Too much *penetration* for anyone to fall asleep. Right?"

"What exactly are you doing on that computer, anyway?"

"Trying to hack it so I can destroy William's stupid company."

"Since when do you know how to hack?"

"I don't," she snapped. "But I know how to guess stupid shit William would use as a password."

We eventually managed to drag Lilith away from the computer, and while she wasn't kicking and screaming, she was giving us looks that rivaled any horror movie villain. If anyone was the person to stab you in your sleep, it was Lilith. I made a mental note to do something nice for her down the line, if only to avoid the whole knife to the face thing.

Driving the car in the costume was difficult, but I managed. I guessed if we got pulled over I'd probably have a hard time talking myself out of a ticket, but considering I was nearly naked beneath the costume, I didn't exactly have a choice since Lilith was in the car.

After I dropped off Lilith, I took Emily to her apartment and walked her to the door.

"Thank you for tonight," she said. "I wasn't sure what to expect, but I definitely didn't expect, well, *this*." She gestured between the two of us.

"Sometimes the unexpected parts are the most fun."

She nodded, but her eyes looked a little sad. "Let's hope so."

I gave her a bit of a confused kiss goodnight, and walked back to my car with her last words playing on repeat in my head. Making a deal to break up with a girl I was rapidly falling for was confusing enough, but trying to decipher her own feelings about the arrangement might as well have been like reading hieroglyphics for me. I guessed the best I could do was try to stop worrying and just enjoy the time I had. After all, I'd had plenty of practice at doomed relationships. This was just the first time I knew when and why it was going to end ahead of time.

15

EMILY

I had to work the morning after the Halloween party, which meant I was bleary-eyed and short on sleep as the seniors for my art class at the retirement home came shuffling into the room. Grammy paused, looked me over, and then gave me a knowing wink.

"Good work, you little hoochie-mamma."

I glared. I was too short on sleep to have the energy for her antics. "Nothing happened. I just didn't get a good night's sleep."

She rolled her eyes and went to sit down near the back, right beside Earl.

It was the second time in less than twenty-four hours that I'd lied about having slept with Ryan. I was never the promiscuous type by any stretch, but I also hadn't felt like I was the type to be secretive about it, either. I was sure there had to be some kind of weird psychological analysis for what I was doing, but if there was, I had no idea.

So I shoved it right down and decided it was a problem for another day. I felt good about last night. The sex had been amazing, for one. And Ryan had been amazing in every other way.

Granted, there was the whole part where he revealed he'd actually been misleading me to a certain extent since the gastropub incident, but other than the knock against how trustworthy he seemed, I couldn't make myself want to dwell on it. He'd admitted it, apologized—and very convincingly, I might add—and now we could move on.

As if thinking about him conjured him up from thin air, Ryan popped into the room with bright eyes and a smile that looked unfairly good on someone I knew had gotten as little sleep as I had.

"Can I sit in?" Ryan asked.

"No," Grammy growled. "Unless you're going to be modeling in the nude for us, and with an erection. I refuse to look at a limp dick for two hours."

"She's not lying," Earl agreed with a grave nod. "She really won't do it."

I winced. I wasn't exactly sure what the story on that could be, but I was sure I didn't want to know.

"He's not modeling nude for us. We're just painting a still-life today and really focusing on three-point perspective."

"Boo," Grammy yelled. "We want penis!"

"Speak for yourself," Earl said in his whispery, thin voice. "I'd take a pair of knockers, though. Unless he's got them under that tight t-shirt, he can keep it on."

Before I could answer, my phone buzzed from inside my purse. I dug it out and looked at the number. It was an area code I didn't recognize, but I excused myself and answered it anyway.

"Hello?"

"Hi, Emily? I'm Valeria Purgot's personal assistant." The woman had a thick, French accent.

My stomach turned ice cold. "Valeria Purgot?" I said dumbly. I knew who she was, of course. She was half the reason I wanted to go to Paris to study. She'd made some of my favorite paintings of all time, and she was teaching part-time as a favor for a year or two at the school I was planning to attend. She was the same one I'd written an embarrassingly candid letter to a little over a month ago.

"Yes. She got your letter, and she thinks you'd be a wonderful apprentice. You'd still be able to attend classes next semester, but she'd be able to offer you paid work starting as soon as you arrived."

"I'm sorry, please don't take this the wrong way, but why would she pick me? And for what kind of work?"

Ryan edged a little closer with a curious but slightly worried expression on his face. I waved him off with a forced smile and mouthed, "it's no big deal."

"Because," the woman said over the phone. "She liked that you took the initiative to send the letter, you're already planning to come for school, which should simplify logistics, and she believes you have potential. Miss Purgot has always had a passion for developing young talent. You would be helping with the day-to-day tasks at her gallery, but she would also provide one-on-one instruction to you."

"When would she need me to arrive by?"

"We would arrange for your flight in two days. Work would begin the following day."

I raised my eyebrows and stared at the wall. "That's... *sudden*."

"Yes. It is. And she will need to know if you're going to accept her offer immediately."

"Immed—can I at least have a few hours to digest all of this?"

"I'm very sorry, but no. It's very important that you would arrive quickly."

"Okay?" I said shakily.

"Very good. We'll be in contact soon with travel arrangements. I'll let Valeria know you've accepted the offer and one of our people will be in touch."

I hung up the phone and looked at Ryan, who was standing beside me with a creased forehead. "What was that?" he asked.

"Let's talk about it after my class, okay? Maybe you can wait outside if you don't mind?"

His expression hardened, and the sight of it made my chest feel tight and empty.

I fumbled and made my way through the class as a distracted mess, and the forty minute session ended up feeling more like two hours. By the time I trailed out of the room after the last of my students, I was feeling every minute of sleep I'd missed catching up with me.

Ryan was sitting in a recliner just outside the room I used, and he hopped to his feet as soon as he saw me. "What was that all about?"

I shook my head but couldn't quite meet his eyes. "I have to go sooner than I thought. I think. I mean, I do. I have to go."

"What? You don't have to be embarrassed about poop stuff with me. If you've gotta go, you've gotta go. I know everyone does it." he laughed, relief cracking through the worry on his face. "Honestly, I'm glad we're getting it out of the way now, because that can always be such an awkward thing. It's like, do I just say I'm taking a leak but disappear for five minutes, or should I be straight up about it?" He searched my face and the relief shifted back into worry. "You're not talking about that. Neither was I, actually. I just didn't want it to be weird for you, so... *shit.* Say something! You're just giving me that look like someone's dead."

I opened my mouth to speak and couldn't think of the right way to put it, so I clamped my lips together and shook my head again. "I don't know what the right choice is here, Ryan. This really big artist apparently wants me to basically be her apprentice. And she wants me to start in two days instead of two months. It'd be a paying job. It'd be my dream, basically, and after feeling like I've been chasing something that wasn't there, it's suddenly falling into my lap." I looked up at him and frowned into those deep, light brown eyes of his as I fought down the waves of emotion threatening to consume me. "What am I supposed to do?"

His eyes fell to the floor as he thought. His expression was somber, and when he finally spoke, it was with the grave determination of someone telling the doctor to amputate their own leg. "You go. Chase the dream."

"Just like that?" I asked. I'd already agreed. It wasn't like I'd signed a contract, but he'd probably heard me agree, and heard how quickly I'd said yes. I couldn't even begin to imagine how that would feel for him, but I knew he couldn't understand how conflicted I felt.

He spread his hands. "What do you want me to say? Stay for me? Stay because I'm so sure it'll be perfect between us? Promise that I'll be more important to you than the thing you've been trying to get your whole life? I can't do any of that. So you go. We had an expiration date, anyway, right?"

"Right," I said softly.

He stuck his hand out like he wanted a handshake.

I stared down incredulously at it. "I guess the whole no hard feelings clause of our agreement went out the window when the expiration date changed?"

"I guess so," he said. His voice sounded cold. Angry, even. When he saw I wasn't going to shake his hand, he turned and walked away.

I watched after him, wanting to crumple in on myself. I couldn't be mad. Why couldn't I ever just be mad at Ryan goddamn Pearson? Why did he always have to be an asshole with some kind of asterisk beside it? Why was there always an excuse in the footnotes: "Ryan was actually just doing what he thought was honorable by protecting his girlfriend, who smeared a cupcake on your senior art project," and "he was only lying to you because he was so worried about losing you," and "he's only mad because he really cared about you, and now he has to let you go."

I sank down and sat against the wall, leaning my head back and letting the fluorescent lights burn rainbow-black, rectangular strips in my vision. I barely noticed when William sat down beside me.

"Looking a little gloomy over here," he said, nudging me with his elbow.

I didn't take my eyes from the ceiling. "Well, your little game as matchmaker looks like it's coming to a fiery end."

"I feel like you're giving me some kind of clue, but it's just not clicking. Can you give me how many syllables I'm looking for?"

"Break up. Two syllables."

"Hmm," he said. "Break up. Break up... It makes me think of ice though, not fire. Like ice breaking up. Ice on fire? No, that's stupid."

I slowly turned to look at him and tried my hardest to figure out if he was stupid or just really good at pushing people's buttons when they shouldn't be pressed. "Ryan and I are breaking up. I have to leave for Paris."

"Wow. Very classic. The old, *gotta leave the country* excuse. I used that one once or twice. Just make sure they don't have relatives in the country you're supposedly migrating to. That can get awkward."

"I'm not making it up."

"Yeah, well," he slapped me on the back, nearly knocking me to the side. "It's too bad there's not a sickeningly rich guy who would be amused to see you two together. Just too bad."

"You know what you're like?"

"Tall, dark, handsome, filthy rich... I could go on, but the look you're giving me is telegraphing *stop*."

"You're like a little kid with two hamsters, and you want them to like each other so you're squishing them together, but you're squishing them so hard together that when you let go, they won't even know how to stay together on their own anymore."

"Wait, that's a really specific example. Did you squish hamsters together when you were a kid? I've always said they shouldn't let kids have pets. They're little psychopaths. I swear."

"I don't know why I'm bothering trying to talk to you. You don't take anything seriously."

"False. Taxes are serious business. Learned that the hard way. I usually take my wife seriously, too. And sunscreen, actually. You'd be shocked if you knew how many people don't even think about it. I feel like I could just list things I'm serious about all day, but you're giving me that look again."

"Why me?" I said. "You could've tried to set Ryan up with anyone, but you picked me. Why?"

"Does it matter now? You said you were ditching the guy. You and I are no longer friends." He stood and dusted his hands. "I owed Ryan a solid, and you spoiled it. If you want to be friends again, I suggest you find a way to make this right."

"Seriously?"

He spread his palms and raised his eyebrows. "See? I can be serious. Yes. And you know what, if you leave, I'll find a hotter version of you. One with—with, really, really big boobs. She won't even be able to tell you what color her shoes are they'll be so big. She'll be the one I set Ryan up with. So while you're finger-painting the Leaning Tower of Pizza, Ryan's going to be motor-boating two flotation devices that could've saved the Titanic from sinking."

"It's the Leaning Tower of *Pisa*, you boob." I made a disgusted sound at him and got up to leave.

"Oh no. I'm the one who gets to storm out of here. This is— hey. I said—hey!" he started fast-walking to keep up with me as I headed for the exit.

I sped up too, but I tried not to make it too obvious. He barely squeezed ahead of me at the door and he closed it in my face, standing outside the glass with a smug look on his face. He dipped his chin at me, spun on his heel, and walked off.

I looked to Cheryl, who was sitting behind the front desk with a strange look on her face. "Don't tell anybody about that. Please."

"Honey, I'm not sure how I'd even describe it. So I think you're safe."

16

RYAN

I slumped against the prep table and stared at the batch of cupcakes I'd just made. They looked horrible. As corny as it sounded, baking wasn't something you should do when you were pissed off, and my cupcakes were a testament to that. They were lopsided, too dry, and I'd decorated them like I had clubs for hands.

"Soo," Stephanie said. She was leaning near the dishwasher as she studied me with her arms crossed. Her hair was held in a bun on top of her head and speared through with what looked like chopsticks. "Are you going to tell me why you just abused those poor cupcakes, or do I have to play detective, like usual?"

"Girl problems," I said.

She nodded. "I don't need to be a detective to know that much. I'm asking what *kind* of girl problems. What happened with you and Emily?"

"It ended is what happened."

"What? I didn't even know it started. What happened to keeping me in the loop?"

"It started last night, and it ended this morning. It's probably a new world record for the shortest relationship ever."

"What did you do?"

I turned to face her. "Who says I did something? I mean, arguably I *did* do some stupid things, but I'd already apologized for those. It was kind of conditional on the relationship starting in the first place. The breakup isn't even my fault."

She looked skeptical. "What did *she* do?"

"She accepted a job halfway across the world without a second thought."

"Does it have something to do with her whole art school thing?"

"Yes," I groaned.

"I thought that was in January."

I sighed. "It was, then it wasn't. But it doesn't matter. She made her choice, and I'm happy for her."

"Yeah," Stephanie said. She picked up one of my cupcakes and turned it around in her hand with a disgusted look on her face. "You look thrilled."

"What am I supposed to do?" I asked. "Be pissed that she cares more about her lifelong dream than some guy she met a couple weeks ago? I can't tell her not to go after this job."

"Who says you can't be pissed?" she asked. Some of her usual hopeless romantic look was starting to creep into her expression. She took a step toward me and jabbed a finger at my chest. "Who says you have to just let her walk out of your life?" Jab. "Who says you can't fight for your woman?" Jab. "Who says," she started, almost yelling now. "Who says you can't go after her! Chase her down in the airport. This is your final act, Ryan. It's the part of the movie where everybody knows the credits are going to roll soon, and they *know* if it was real life, you would just let her walk, because that's what normal people do. But they are watching a freaking movie, so they know you're going to do something extraordinary, something that inspires them, and they're going to cheer for you the whole way."

I threw my hands up and looked around the bakery. "One

problem. No cameras here. In your little scenario, they also know the girl would never turn down the guy. They know whatever dumb stunt he pulls is going to work. What happens if I chase her through the airport and she just looks at me like I'm an idiot?"

"Then you know you tried, and you don't have to stand here abusing cupcakes for the next few months until you finally get over her. Except you'll never *really* get over her. You'll see hints of her in every woman you ever talk to if you let her go. You'll wake up in a cold sweat wondering *what if.* You'll—"

"I get it. I do, really. And..." I looked at her and groaned. "As much as I hate admitting this to you, I was already planning on a stupid stunt. Okay?"

"You're going to get her pregnant," she whispered in stunned reverie, like it was the most genius idea she'd ever heard."

"What? No. The cupcakes. They're part of the stupid stunt. Except not these ones, because they turned out horrible."

Stephanie's eyes lit up. "Oh. My. God. How can I help?"

AGAINST MY BETTER JUDGMENT, I LET STEPHANIE CONTRIBUTE SOME ideas to my grand scheme. As a result, it had somehow spiraled into a complicated, theatrical event that involved me, Stephanie, Steve, Bruce, Natasha, William, Hailey, and even Grammy.

We all met in William's massive apartment at five in the morning. Everybody looked dressed and ready to go, except William, who wore a fuzzy, white bathrobe and kept yawning.

"I'm going to go over it one last time so everyone knows their job," I said. I pointed at a map I'd printed out of the city. I'd high-lighted Emily's apartment and the quickest path to the airport. William had threatened to fire Lilith if she didn't do some digging and find out what time Emily's flight was, so we knew a rough window of when she'd be leaving. I tapped the spot where I had her apartment marked. "Bruce and Natasha, you're the lookouts in her apartment lobby. Wear a disguise or something so she doesn't spot you, and then text me as soon as you see her leave."

"I'm not wearing a disguise," Bruce said. He bit into the banana he was holding and chewed mechanically while he watched me with those cold eyes of his.

Natasha nudged him. "We've got that police officer outfit, from the honeymoon."

Bruce's jaw flexed, and I could've sworn I saw red creep into his cheeks.

William did a comically slow turn toward his brother with wide-eyed delight. "Officer Bruce? Why is it so easy to picture that?" He barked out a laugh.

Hailey covered her mouth beside him and kept sneaking glances at Bruce, who was now chewing into his banana with studied ferocity.

"Well," I said, barely keeping laughter from my own voice. "A police officer might be a bit too conspicuous. It'd also probably be best if you weren't sexually aroused. I'll need you to focus."

Bruce gave me a glare that could've melted steel beams. "No costume," he said coldly.

"Just try to stay out of sight," I said.

Natasha was still grinning at Bruce. She slid her arm behind his back and I saw him give a little, surprised jump like she'd pinched his butt. When he thought no one was watching, he gave her a very meaningful stare that said she was probably going to pay for that, and they were both going to enjoy the punishment.

"Steve, you're going to wait at the corner here. If traffic is bad, she might actually go a different route, and we need to know if she's going to make it to the bridge or not. If she goes straight, you text me 'good,' if she goes left, you text me 'bad.' Okay?"

He pursed his lips. "I was thinking code words would be better. What if she intercepts the texts or something? I could say 'The condor flies true' for her going straight. And I could say, like, 'Westerly winds prevail' if she goes left."

"Left would be Easterly winds," William said. He tapped the map to show Steve what he was talking about.

"Oh shit, you're right. Okay, 'Easterly winds prevail,' then."

"Actually," Hailey said. "I'm pretty sure condors aren't native here. Maybe an Osprey would make more sense?"

"*Actually*," I said. "Maybe we could just stick with good and bad? Who the hell is going to intercept a text?"

Steve pulled a face. "You'd be surprised. *You'd be surprised.*"

"Somehow I don't think I would. Just make sure you text me which way she goes, okay?"

"That's a big ten-four," he said.

"And no more code talk."

"Copy that."

I sighed. "William and Hailey. You two are going to wait at her gate in the airport to run distraction if I don't get there in time. Find a way to stall her if I text you. If not, just browse a gift shop or something, I don't care."

"Sounds easy, got it," said William.

"And Grammy, you get a ticket." I handed her a ticket for the flight Emily was taking. "If everything goes wrong and she manages to get on the plane, you're my last resort. You make a scene and get the flight delayed. Bonus points if you can get everyone off the plane."

Grammy studied the ticket, then nodded. "Gucci."

I groaned. "Do kids even say that one, anymore?"

She shrugged. "Why, am I making you uncomfortable, *bitch?*"

I was torn between laughing and shaking my head in annoyance, but settled on ignoring her comment.

William reached out to fist bump her. "Nice," he whispered.

She side-eyed his fist and then crossed her arms.

"Asshole," he muttered.

"What's my job?" Stephanie asked.

"Half of this was your idea. Do you really need me to tell you again?"

She pouted a little. "I wanted to feel like part of the team."

"Okay. Your job is to go get the cupcakes when we're done here and meet me at the bridge with them."

"Got it!" She half-shouted, then cleared her throat and spoke again, much more quietly this time. "Got it."

"Then it's a plan," I said. "Let's do this."

17

EMILY

I sat on the edge of my bed for thirty minutes longer than I had time to. It was already six in the morning, and I needed to be out of the apartment in less than an hour. Every time I thought of getting off the bed, my stupid brain decided to play a mopey highlight reel of all my moments with Ryan. I saw his dazzling smile, those gorgeous pools of brown he calls eyes, and the way his butt looked in my Bill of Rights costume.

It was easier if I thought of his cold dismissal yesterday morning. Yes, I'd probably made it sound like I was jumping at the chance to take the job without even considering him, but I also didn't think it would've killed him to put up a little more of a fight. It seemed like he was high school Ryan all over again, doing the thing he thought was noble and right, but he was ending the relationship in the process. I couldn't put that on him, though. I was the one leaving. It was my dream that had put a wrench in everything.

I only wished I knew which dream was the one worth sacrificing everything for.

I moped out of bed and into the shower. Then I moped to the mirror and did the *I'm-only-running-into-the-gas-station-and-*

coming-straight-home level of makeup and hair on myself. I slid into an oversized hoodie, sweatpants, and then grabbed my luggage. I either looked like a celebrity trying to be incognito, or a homeless person who stole somebody's suitcase.

I headed through the lobby without even looking around and taking in everything one last time. I hadn't actually canceled my lease yet or done the final cleaning out of my apartment, but Lilith had surprisingly agreed to help handle that once I was gone so I wouldn't have to rush to get everything finished.

It was colder outside than I expected, so I flipped up the hood on my hoodie and almost didn't see Lilith until she was right on top of me.

"Hey, loser," she said. "I was going to give you a ride."

"Oh. I already called an Uber."

"Whatever. I didn't want to drive you there, anyway."

"I mean, I can—"

"No. It's fine." Lilith hesitated. She looked to the side and rolled her tongue across the inside of her cheek. "Look. I'm going to miss you, even though you're an idiot."

"I'm going to miss you too," I said. I stepped forward and gave her a tight hug. The last time Lilith had allowed me to hug her was all the way back in middle school when I'd found her crying by herself in the girl's bathroom. "But you know I'm coming back," I said over her shoulder. "It'll just be two years."

She slowly brought her arms up and gave me a small squeeze. "Yeah, whatever. I'll be, like, counting the days on my calendar." Her voice was laced with sarcasm, but when I pulled back, her eyes looked a little watery. "I'm leaving. Better things to do than sit around here and let you fondle me." She took a step away, paused, then gave my shoulder a little punch before heading back to her car and driving off.

I got in my Uber just in time to see Bruce and Natasha Chamberson walking out of my apartment building. I squinted in confusion, but was sure it was them. Natasha pointed after Lilith's car, then Bruce nodded. He looked down at his phone and started texting someone. I was still trying to figure out what that could've meant when my driver started heading for the airport. He was the professional kind of Uber driver—the kind who had water bottles and all kinds of snacks and hand sanitizer available for his passengers. He had papers plastered everywhere about how much he appreciated good reviews. Thankfully, he also wasn't the talkative type, as I was more in the mood to stare out the window and feel sorry for myself.

Tomorrow, I could shift gears and focus on how awesome it was that I had this opportunity, but I was designating today as my mopey day.

I sat up straighter a few minutes later when I could've sworn I saw Ryan's roommate standing on the street corner. He was chatting with three girls who looked like tourists while shadowing a football throwing motion.

"I know a quicker way to the airport from here," the driver said. "We'll save five minutes. Guaranteed. You can write about that in your review." He looked up in the rearview to give me a wink.

I sat back in my seat and watched the city pass by for the rest of the drive. It was strange thinking about how long I'd be away from New York, which had been such a huge part of my life. When I'd called my parents and given them an update yesterday, they were encouraging. Still, I couldn't fight the lump in my stomach that made me feel like I was getting it wrong.

I got out of the car at the airport, grabbed my luggage, and thanked the driver. I made it through the airport without any incidents, except seeing a couple I could've sworn was William and Hailey Chamberson in one of the gift shops. I did a double-take, but I was on one of those walking escalators and didn't have time to get off and go look to see if it was really them. Besides, William and I had left off on an awkward note, so even if it was him, I doubted he'd have been glad to see me.

When they called for us to board the plane, I guiltily stole a glance behind me. Some dumb, romantic part of my brain hoped I'd see Ryan come running through the terminal to stop me from boarding the plane. One last, desperate act of love. I heard a commotion in the distance and actually stopped, letting a few people pass me in line. My back straightened and I strained my eyes to see what it was.

William Chamberson was running and laughing at the top of his lungs as two out-of-shape security guards tried to catch him. He was holding an "I Love New York" t-shirt in his hand that still had the tag on it. He turned a corner and the sound of his laughter trailed away. A few seconds later, I saw Hailey following with her arms crossed and an embarrassed look on her face.

I turned back to the line with a heavy breath, gave my ticket, and boarded the flight.

At least I had a window seat, even if the majority of my view was going to be the ocean. I'd never even flown internationally before, so *that* was exciting. Sort of.

I was just getting settled in my seat when I heard something thud into the window. I looked, expecting to see a bird falling away, but didn't see anything. A second later, there was another thud, and I saw bright orange frosting smeared across my window.

18

NATASHA, STEVE, AND WILLIAM

One Hour Earlier

Natasha

WE WAITED IN THE LOBBY OF EMILY'S BUILDING NOT LONG AFTER our top-secret meeting in William's apartment. I felt giddy with excitement.

"This is so cool. It's kind of like Ocean's Eleven, you know? Except instead of stealing a fortune we're helping Ryan steal someone's heart."

The corner of Bruce's mouth twitched in amusement. "That's one way of looking at it."

"What's another?"

"That Ryan could've much more easily just called her and asked her to meet for a few minutes so they could talk."

I sighed. "Where would be the romance in that?"

"It would be practical."

"Maybe you could use a lesson in romantic gestures," I said a little flippantly.

He cocked his head at me and grinned. "Maybe if you hadn't decided to talk about the roleplay in the bedroom in front of everyone earlier, I'd be more open to the idea."

I laughed. "Come on. You have to admit their reactions were funny."

"Emotionally scarring, yes. Funny, no."

"Agree to disagree."

He looked at his watch. "Isn't she supposed to be—"

"There!" I said. "Shh. Act discreet."

Bruce stood as still as a statue, which, admittedly, was probably his best attempt at being discreet. I half-turned my face and watched her from the corner of my eye.

"Okay!" I whispered once she left. "She's outside, we've got to follow!"

"What?" asked Bruce. "Our job was just to text when she left." He pulled out his phone like he was about to text and I tried to swipe it from his hand to stop him. He easily dodged my hand, which made me lose my balance. My arms pinwheeled and I ended up face planting into the floor. At least I would have if something hadn't caught my jacket and had me floating half an inch from the floor.

Bruce lifted me up by the back of my jacket and placed me back on my feet. "Any reason you were trying to knock my phone away?"

"We have to make sure she gets in the car!" I tugged on his arm and made him come outside with me. I just had time to see Lilith getting in her car and pulling away from the curb, but the way the sky was reflecting off her window made it almost impossible to see if Emily was in the passenger seat.

"Try to get a look and see if she's in there!" I said.

Bruce and I moved toward the street but couldn't quite get an angle on the car. I sighed. "Fine. You can text that she left."

Steve

I PUT A HAND AGAINST THE TRAFFIC SIGNAL AND GRINNED AT THE tourists. They were cute. The middle one was my favorite because she was nailing the whole church girl gone bad look. But the other two weren't slouches, either, and as a bonus, they were all tourists. Something about girls on trips together seemed to be a sure-fire sign that they were down for threesomes or foursomes.

"Yeah," I said. "I'm basically a step away from making the roster. Just a few injuries at the right time, and boom. I'm there."

"Wow." The church girl gone bad batted her eyelashes. "I can't wait to tell all my friends we met an NFL quarterback."

The other two bobbed their heads in eager agreement.

Some guys would say it was too easy. Not enough of a challenge. But what the hell did they know? If I was going fishing and I had to choose between a fishing rod and a grenade, I wasn't about to waste my afternoon pulling them up one by one. Hell no. You pull out the big guns and you let those puppies roar.

"They say I've got one of the quickest releases they've ever seen," I said, shadowing my drop back and passing motion. "But that's just on the field," I added with a smirk. "When the lights are off, I'm kind of known for how long I can last before I release."

They all giggled.

In the back of my head, I felt like I was forgetting something, but I couldn't really be bothered to remember. All I knew was that I was about to score. *Three times.*

William

"THIS IS THE WORST GIFT SHOP I'VE EVER SEEN," I SAID.

Hailey gave a little shrug. "I don't know. These little guys are kind of cute, don't you think?" She slid a Yankee's cap on her head and did a little pose.

"The model is fantastic," I said, stepping in and squeezing her ass despite her embarrassed glances over her shoulder. "But the selection? Not so much."

She put the hat back and moved to look at a display of mugs with names on them. "Time to see if they have my name..."

"If they don't, we burn the place down."

She gave me a sharp look. "You shouldn't joke about things like that, because I still haven't figured out when you're being serious and when you're joking."

I plucked a fake statue of liberty torch from the shelf and acted like I was holding it to a stack of postcards. I gave her a suggestive wiggle of my eyebrows.

She turned around, unimpressed.

"Should we be keeping an eye out, or something?" she asked.

"No. Bruce texts Ryan. Ryan texts Steve. Steve texts Ryan. Ryan texts us. That's the order, and we haven't been texted. That means the eagle has not landed."

"What if there's some kind of technical glitch and the text doesn't come through?"

"Well," I said. "Then Mr. Romeo is going to have to sit his over-dramatic ass on an airplane and go to Paris, isn't he?"

She glared. "Aren't you the one who orchestrated this whole thing in the first place?"

"I am the evil genius that gave birth to this monstrosity, yes."

"Shouldn't you maybe be more involved in helping fix it then? Or at least act like you care?"

"I did my part. I ignited the flames. Sometimes it's just not meant to be, Hailey. Not everybody is as magnetic as you and I."

She rolled her eyes, but gave me half of a smile. "Yeah, you're magnetic all right, because you stuck to me and I can't seem to find a way to get you off."

I turned her to face me and tilted her chin up. "That's the most romantic thing you've ever said to me."

"Oh?" she asked, biting her lip.

"Yes, now I'm going to need you to check my pole to see if it's charged."

She shook her head. "I wish I knew enough about magnets to tell you if that was even a good or bad pun."

"You're getting me all excited with your sass. I'm either going to have to take advantage of you, or steal something."

"We're supposed to be doing a job," she said. "What if I promise you as soon as this is over—"

"Nope," I said. I gave her a quick kiss. "I've always wanted one of these t-shirts, you know." I pulled an "I Love New York" t-shirt off the rack and gave her a dangerous grin.

"No, William. Seriously. We're supposed to—"

"Don't be a tight-ass. I'm going to give it back if they catch me. And if they don't, I'll totally reverse-steal it."

"William," she warned.

"Sorry!" I kissed her one more time and took off for the exit of the gift shop, laughing maniacally as I went.

19

RYAN

I sat in my parked car by the bridge Emily was supposed to be crossing with my phone in my hand. I'd scrutinized every single car and was sure I hadn't seen Lilith's yet. Based on when Bruce sent his text letting me know Emily left, I should've already heard from Steve. I glanced at the time once more and then dialed Steve's number.

"What's up?" he sounded hesitant, like he knew he'd done something wrong.

"You tell me," I said slowly.

I heard girls giggling in the background through the phone and my stomach sunk. "I got distracted, but I've been watching pretty good ever since."

"So she might have already passed you?"

"I mean, anything is possible. She might be a lizard in a skin suit for all we—"

I hung up and narrowed my eyes. It was Lilith's car. I turned the ignition and started to drive. The bridge wasn't heavily trafficked, which worked in my favor because I was able to pull my car in front of her lane to block off the bridge while still giving her enough time to stop.

She still screeched to a stop with just inches to spare before hitting my car.

I got out, grabbed the cupcake from my back seat, and walked toward her car. I couldn't see if Emily was in the passenger seat because of the headlights, but Bruce shouldn't have texted if she wasn't.

The driver-side door opened and Lilith stepped out with a confused expression on her face. Behind her, cars were starting to clog the bridge and honk. I hadn't thought about the noise when I was imagining the perfect romantic gesture, but that was fine. I could apologize later.

"Emily!" I had to yell to be heard over the honking horns.

"Ryan!" Lilith yelled. "She's not here, dumbass."

"What?"

"She took an Uber. I guess she wanted to start off her new chapter all by herself, or whatever." Lilith shrugged. "I was going to drive up there and just make sure her plane doesn't explode on the runway, I guess."

"Shit. When did she leave?"

"Right after me. Hey, is that cupcake for me? Because I skipped breakfast."

I ignored her and ran back to my car, carefully putting the cupcake in the tray with the rest and then jumping behind the wheel. I drove as fast as I could to the airport.

When I arrived, I parked in the area that was probably going to get me ticketed or even towed, grabbed the tray of a dozen cupcakes I'd baked, and hurried inside. I tried to walk straight to the gates, but a police officer stopped me short.

"Sir," he said. "I can't let you in here with those."

"They're cupcakes," I said. "And I'm kind of in a hurry." I was trying not to lose my cool, but I knew Emily could already be boarding the plane, and I didn't have time to waste.

"In a hurry, are you? Planning to blow something up? I could slap the gloves on and we could start with a cavity search."

"Are you serious? You see a tray of cupcakes and your first thought is sticking your fingers up my ass?"

"It's your choice."

"Then I choose the option that doesn't involve penetration."

He spread his palms and watched me go with a self-satisfied smirk as I headed outside without a plan. I looked down at the tray, sucked in a breath, and then started shoving cupcakes in my jacket pockets. I only fit about seven before I was at risk of looking like I'd, well, shoved a bunch of cupcakes in my pockets. It was butchering the perfect moment I was envisioning, and definitely changing my plans, but it didn't seem that I had a choice, so I swallowed my annoyance and headed back inside.

The same guard took a step toward me. "What happened to the treats?"

"Saw a hungry homeless guy," I said. "Sorry, no butt stuff for you today, I guess."

"Yeah, well maybe I'll radio ahead to TSA and see what they have to say about that."

I ignored him and pressed forward. I hoped he was bluffing, but given the luck I'd already had so far, I couldn't really count on it.

I kept scanning the crowd for Emily as I half-jogged toward her gate. I tried calling William and then Hailey, but got no answer. Like the rest of my "team," they were useless.

I waited impatiently in the line for security, and somehow managed to squeeze through without anyone wondering why I was standing so awkwardly. I could feel the icing staining through my shirt and sticking to my skin beneath my jacket, but I pressed on, even though my modified plan was feeling dumber and dumber by the minute.

I jogged as fast as I could without jostling the cupcakes loose or drawing the attention of more security. By the time I made it to her gate, the door was already shut and nobody seemed to be waiting to board.

Shit.

I scanned the area until I saw an airport employee dragging a luggage train and wearing an orange vest.

"Hey," I said, tapping his shoulder.

He stopped and gave me a confused look.

"I need to get down to the runway."

The man looked at me with infinite patience and nodded. He was in his early twenties and built like a lanky bird. "We have a procedure for that, sir. You wait for your flight, get on your plane, and then you're on the runway."

"No, I need to get my feet on the runway, as soon as humanly possible."

"That's not allowed."

"What if I bribe you? A hundred dollars. Just give me your vest and show me a door I can take to get down there.

He pursed his lips. "I want those shoes. They're nice, and you look about my size. Thirteen?"

"My shoes? Fine, whatever, yes. Thirteen and a half, but they're yours."

"I'll need to see the cash…"

I dug the money out of my wallet and handed it to him.

"Shoes?"

I sighed, kicked off my shoes, and slid them toward him. He slowly took his own off and then tried mine, flexing his toes once they were on. "Very nice." He dug in his pocket, pulled out a high-lighter, and streaked it across each of the twenties I'd given him. "Looks legit."

"You seriously have a counterfeit pen on you? How often do you take bribes?"

"You'd be surprised. People like to bring weird shit in their luggage and they don't want it getting scanned. Now come on, the stairs are over here."

Nobody gave us a second look as we descended the stairs.

They opened onto the runway, which was freezing cold and windy once we were outside.

"Dude, wait," he said, gripping my shoulder. "Are those cupcakes in your jacket?"

"Yes," I groaned. "I'm in a hurry."

"Then give me one."

"They're all warm and squashed beca—"

"I don't care. I'm hungry."

I fished out a flattened cupcake and peeled it from my undershirt. He took it and bit into it with an approving nod. "You make these?"

I shook my head in disbelief. "Which plane would she be on? It was gate 8, seat 42."

"That one," he said, pointing to the nearest plane. "She should be on the right side of the plane, I think,"

I set off at a jog again, pinning my jacket to my side to avoid losing any more cupcakes as I ran. I ran to the right side of the plane and picked a window at random near the middle. I chucked the cupcake as hard as I could and watched it splatter between two windows. A middle-aged man glared down at me from the window, but I saw a face pop up just behind his. *It was her.*

I wound up and threw another cupcake directly for her window. It splattered dead-center, but had the unintended side-effect of making me clueless to what she was doing. I pulled out my phone, which was covered in icing because it had shared storage space with a cupcake, and I dialed Grammy's number.

20

EMILY

Ryan just threw a cupcake at my window. I craned my neck to look out the window behind me and saw him standing there on the runway. He was wearing a bright orange safety vest over his long jacket, and it looked like he had the same colored orange icing smeared all over his clothes. Confused didn't even begin to describe what I was feeling.

It only got worse when I heard a familiar voice a few seats back.

"Excuse me," asked a sweet sounding, little old woman's voice.

Grammy was inexplicably standing from her seat. On my plane. All the unlikely coincidences so far this morning combined with Ryan on the runway told me something was going on, but I couldn't even begin to guess what it was.

"Now," Grammy said to the stewardess she had stopped. "I'm not saying I have a bomb. But I'm just asking, if someone did say they had a bomb on the plane, would it delay our flight?"

The stewardess looked extremely uncomfortable, and her eyes kept darting toward the front of the plane, where two other stewardesses were standing and talking. "Y-yes. That would mean we would have to delay the flight."

"Wait," Grammy clutched at her chest. "Actually, no, I think I'm having a heart attack." The stewardess, who was clearly confused out of her mind, half-reached toward Grammy and then decided to loudly call for help.

During the chaos, Grammy slid her eyes to mine and gave me a wink before flopping to the ground and swearing up a storm about who she was going to come back to haunt and how "heaven gon' be lit."

Between the people who were watching Grammy with mixtures of horror and bewilderment and the people who were trying to figure out who would throw a cupcake at an airplane, chaos was in full swing

For my part, all I could do was stay where I was and stare at the orange frosting smeared across my window. Why would he be here? Why would Grammy be on my flight? *Why cupcakes?* Obviously I was in the middle of a plan, and I was out of the loop. If I'd had a quiet place to sit down and think, I was sure I could've figured it out, but I felt suffocated and claustrophobic.

A few minutes later, a group of EMTs rushed on the plane with a stretcher. The last man in the group was *Ryan.* He'd ditched the orange safety vest for an EMT jacket that was much too big for him, but nobody seemed to notice he'd just slapped it on over his jacket and pants.

He motioned for me to follow him. Meanwhile, I could hear Grammy cursing at the EMTs to stop molesting her unless they had good insurance, because they could bet their tight asses she was going to sue.

Ryan stopped me just outside the airplane in the tunnel. He was covered in sweat and grinning like a crazy person.

"Can you please tell me what the hell is going on?" I asked.

"Next time," he said, "I'm just going to text. But I had this whole thing planned." He held up a hand for me to wait and fished around inside his jacket. His hand made a wet, squishing sound that had me cringing, but he ended up pulling out a mangled cupcake with orange frosting. A piece of paper was stuck in it and completely coated in smeared chocolate and frosting.

"It's, well," he sighed, rubbing some of the frosting off on his pants and holding it up for me to see. "It's a plane ticket. I may have to get a replacement, but the plan was to catch you on the bridge. I was going to give you a cupcake with the plane ticket in it."

I motioned to the plane. "I already had a ticket... And why a cupcake?"

He sighed a little impatiently. "No, like. A ticket for me. To Paris."

"What?"

"A ticket for me. To Paris," he repeated."

"I heard you," I laughed. "I just—that's crazy. You've got all your shops here. And I appreciate the gesture, but be realistic. I'm going to be in Paris for two years. What are you going to do, stay a few weeks? It doesn't change anything, even if it's sweet."

"Considering the Bubbly Baker is expanding to Paris, I wouldn't say I'll exactly be a stranger. I'm the self-appointed foreign business manager, too, which means my ass is on the line if we don't get some franchises overseas soon."

I tilted my head. "Your ass is on the line to who, exactly?"

"To whom," he corrected. "And I'd be reporting to myself, technically. But I promoted Stephanie, and William promised he'd help, since he kind of got this whole thing started, I figured it was the least he could do."

"Well," I said slowly. "It's just too bad we broke up, then, because it's going to be hard for you to find a new girl in France when you don't even speak the language."

"I was hoping that part was negotiable. The break-up."

"Oh?" I asked. I was managing to keep my composure, but my heart was thudding violently in my chest. I was still playing mental catch up, but my heart had no doubts about what it wanted. All this time I'd been seeing Ryan as one of two doors. He was option "B" and chasing my dream was option "A." I'd never even considered a world where I could have both, because what man in his right mind would follow a girl he just met to Paris, especially when he'd be leaving behind a rapidly growing business empire.

"What do you say, new deal?" he asked. "Last time, I promised I'd let you go when the time came, no strings attached. I have a new offer."

"I'm listening."

"This time, I don't let you go, no matter what. Okay, actually, that sounded kind of wrong. I mean, if you wanted me to, obviously, but—"

I rocked forward on my tiptoes and kissed him. "Deal."

He grinned with a wonderfully stunned look on his face.

"You never explained what the deal was with the cupcakes, or why you seemed to think it was necessary to smear them all over your body."

"It was symbolic," he said a little sadly. "I mean, not the smearing on my body part. That was more because of a security guard who had a fixation with putting things up my butt."

"Uh, should I be jealous, or do I even want to know?"

"No. You're way cuter than he was," he said. "But I messed things up the first time with a cupcake, kind of, at least. I wanted to fix them with a cupcake. Full circle and all that."

I looked at the mangled bits of baked goods covering him and the sad excuse for a cupcake in his hand. I swiped my finger across the icing and licked it from my finger with a little smirk. "From the looks of things, I don't know if perfectly executed plans are in your DNA, but I'd be happy to come along for the messy ride." I paused, then put my fingers to my lip and felt my smirk widen. "That actually sounded really dirty. Sorry?"

"Please don't be, and I'm going to hold you to that. The messy ride bit."

Just as he was finishing his sentence, the EMTs came from the plane with a struggling Grammy between their arms. "Get it, girl," she cackled. "Don't worry about me! My grandson-in-law is a raving mad billionaire. He'll bail me out of this jam."

We watched her kick and shake her way down the tunnel in the hands of the EMTs, then Ryan turned back to face me. "So, uh, I also couldn't manage to get a flight for today. So I'll actually have to meet up with you tomorrow."

I laughed. "This plan of yours really just didn't go like you wanted, did it?"

He sighed. "No. But the most important part did."

I kissed him again. "You can be cheesy. But it's a good kind of cheesy."

From the stupid smile on his face, he was about to say something dumb. "Would you go as far as to say it's a Gouda kinda cheesy?"

I rolled my eyes and laughed. "Leave the horrible puns to William. Speaking of William, I'm pretty sure he was getting chased through the airport by security for shoplifting. I don't know if he's going to be able to bail Grammy out as quickly as she was hoping."

"That explains why I didn't get a text when you showed up."

"Okay, you're seriously going to have to sit me down and explain how complicated this failed plan of yours was."

"Is this before or after the messy ride you're going to take on me?"

I wiggled my eyebrows. "After?"

He kissed me this time, and he held his lips against mine in a soft, tender kind of way before he pulled back and gave me that smile of his that made me want to melt on the spot. "You'd better get back on your flight. I've got some loose ends to tie up, and then I'll meet you in Paris."

"It sounds so romantic when you say it that way."

"Good. At least one part of this went romantically instead of comically wrong."

He gripped my hand and squeezed it. "Don't let them crash the plane."

"I'll do my best. And when you get to Paris, maybe you should just call me? No grand stunts or anything. I don't know if I'd trust you to survive another complicated plan."

"Deal."

21

EPILOGUE - RYAN

Three Weeks Later

It took a lot more work than I was expecting when I hatched the idea at the last minute, but I finally closed my first deal on a Paris franchise location for The Bubbly Baker. Emily spent almost more time working than me. She busy with her new position with Valeria Purgot, but we were sharing an apartment, which meant I still had plenty of time to enjoy her.

We had a modest little place on the edge of the city, and for once, a small apartment didn't mean bumping elbows with Steve —instead, I was bumping entirely different body parts with Emily. All in all, it was much more enjoyable this way.

It was evening, and Emily was leaning over our balcony, taking in the view of the city. She had already established a habit of wandering toward the windows, and I'd quickly learned to love just watching her here. At first, I'd wondered if her insatiable need to drink in the city with her eyes at every opportunity was going to pass in a few days, but she was still just as taken with the city as my first day with her here.

She wore a classic little white dress with a black polka dot pattern. It was girlier than her usual style, but it still had her signature dash of quirky. I admired her while she admired the city. It wasn't just how well she wore the dress or the way the wind teased her long hair. I admired how determined she was to chase the dream that led her here. She was willing to sacrifice everything for it, and even though I knew I was one of those sacrifices, it made being here with her mean even more.

She wasn't like any of the women I'd ever dated before because she had her own purpose in life, with or without me. She knew where she was going and how she wanted to get there. I wasn't the answer to her problems or the path to her dreams. She didn't *need* me, and that made the fact that she wanted me here matter.

I moved to join her on the balcony and slid my arm around her waist. "I like watching you out here."

"Creep," she laughed.

"Sorry, you bring out the stalker in me, I guess. Did I mention you looked great while you were sleeping last night?"

She lightly rammed her shoulder into me and smiled. "Thank you."

"I was kidding. I mean, I'm sure you looked great, but—"

"No, I'm not talking about that. I mean thank you for not giving up on me. I haven't been able to stop looking back on how it all played out, how easy it would've been for you let me go and forget me."

"I'm glad I didn't, because then I never would've had the chance to hear how horrible you are at karaoke."

She slapped my arm. "Yeah, well our kids would be doomed, because you sound like—" She paused, swallowed hard, and then cleared her throat. "Ever wish you had a five-second time machine?"

I laughed. "No, but I'm glad you don't have one. Now I know you're already thinking about the kids we'll have."

She made a pouting face and hid behind her hands. "This is the part where I become the overly attached girlfriend meme, isn't it?"

"No. It's the part where I start imagining how much fun I'd have putting babies inside of you."

"Wait, like, literally, or do you just mean in sperm form?"

"Way to drain the sexy right out of that statement."

22

EPILOGUE - EMILY

～

I t was my first Thanksgiving outside the country. I still wasn't sure how to feel about it. Paris was wonderful and amazing, but it wasn't home.

Ryan was doing his best to distract me, but I'd spent much of the day feeling a little off. We were walking on a grassy pathway outside a busy little street crowded with shops. Ryan looked amazing, as usual, in a white button-down with the sleeves rolled up. When we rounded a corner, I saw a large table sitting beneath a pair of trees and stopped in my tracks.

Almost everyone from back home was sitting at the table: William, Hailey, Bruce, Natasha, Lilith, and even Grammy.

"Wow," I said. "Did you do this?"

Ryan gave me a little smirk and a shrug. "That depends. Are you happy?"

"Yes!" I laughed.

"Okay, then it was me. Seriously, William?" Ryan asked when he saw William had already loaded his plate full of food and was eating. I had a little speech I was going to give.

Everybody groaned.

Ryan and I found our places at the table without any big ceremony or awkward pause, like we'd just come in from the kitchen instead of wandering upon the table in the middle of a park in downtown Paris.

I sat between Lilith and Ryan, and once we were seated, everybody started helping themselves. The food was mostly in to-go style containers, and while there were a few staple Thanksgiving items like a turkey and cranberry sauce, there were also a few bits of French cuisine sprinkled in like baguettes and croissants.

"Were you serious about the speech?" I asked Ryan quietly.

"No, definitely not." He answered a little too quickly, and I thought his cheeks looked rosy, too.

I nudged him. "Were you going to talk about pilgrims?"

"Keep teasing me and I'll make you listen to the pilgrim speech in bed tonight instead of letting you experience the Thanksgiving miracle I had planned."

I laughed and darted my eyes nervously around the table. Everybody was chatting or admiring the view, and thankfully not paying much attention to us. "And that is?"

"Well, it's the after dark turkey stuffing ceremony."

"Like leftovers at night?"

"No, like I call you a turkey and then we have sex. The turkey gets stuffed. I say thanks. Bada bing, bada boom."

"One, never say 'bada bing, bada boom' again, or I'm going to get you deported. Two, if you call me a turkey, you're not getting lucky tonight."

He jabbed a honeyed carrot from a tinfoil tray and popped it in his mouth. "We'll see about that, turkey."

I stomped on his foot a little, but he only grinned.

"So," Lilith said. "Now that you two are done making plans to bone, are you going to say hi to your friend that you haven't seen in forever, or, you know, just keep ignoring me?"

I gave Lilith a one-armed hug and kissed the top of her head.

"Ew," she said dryly. "I didn't ask you to touch me."

"Well, too bad. I'm excited to see you."

"Yeah, well, I'm glad your plane didn't crash or whatever."

"What is it like working for Valeria Purgot?" Natasha asked. She sat beside Bruce, and the two of them seemed the most interested in the view of the city. I also noticed that Bruce had a banana on his plate, even though I didn't see where he would've found it among the Thanksgiving food.

"It's hard, but kind of awesome," I said. "She's a total perfectionist, but she's really savvy with the commercial side of art. She's all about how you can chase your passion and still find a way to put food on the table."

"Here's how you put food on the table," Grammy said. "Seduction. The power of the vagina. Suppress the man's will to resist. Overcome his--"

"That's probably enough, Grammy," Hailey said softly. "This is Thanksgiving, not a Communist rally."

William bulged his eyes in delight and held his hand out for Hailey to fist-bump him. She discreetly pushed her small fist against his.

Grammy gave Hailey a side eye, then took an impressive bite out of her turkey leg. "Well," she said through a mouthful of food. "Deny the power between your legs all you want. Just means more for me."

William tilted his head. "I'm not sure you really thought that statement through."

She pointed her fork at him from across the table. "And I'm not sure you want another ass-whooping for back talking me, do you, boy?"

"You fought dirty, and I was drunk. *And* I was just doing the gentlemanly thing by letting you win."

"Pussy," she said with a sideways smile.

William glared.

We finished the rest of the meal without much drama, except for an occasional fight between William and Grammy or a teasing match between Bruce and William. It was the first time since I'd arrived in Paris that I *wanted* to stop absorbing the views around me and the new experience. I let my mind close off to everything but the familiar sounds of the people I'd quickly come to think of as part of my family, and I felt like I was home again.

RYAN AND I WERE BY OURSELVES IN THE APARTMENT A FEW HOURS later after saying our goodbyes and wishing everyone well before their trips back home. I still couldn't quite believe they'd all managed to fly to Paris just to have Thanksgiving dinner with us, but then I remembered William and Bruce probably had private jets and probably hardly thought twice about the expense of flying everyone over.

Ryan was typing up an email on his laptop at the kitchen table, and he was making his concentration face that I always thought was so sexy. I moved up behind him and hugged his neck. "Thank you for today. It was like you knew how bad I'd need that little dose of home."

He kissed my arm. It was such a casual gesture, but it made me feel warm all over. In a lot of ways, it almost scared me how quickly I'd fallen into feeling somehow like an old couple with him but also having the fireworks every time we touched. It was the best of both worlds. The comfort and ease of an old, well-worn relationship where you never had to worry about being judged or hiding who you were, but I still laid awake every night giddy with the thought that he was mine and I was his--that despite all the odds, we'd found a way to make it work.

He'd shown another side of himself since coming here, too. He was more supportive of my dream than I could've ever hoped for. He admired me and appreciated my passion, regardless of how many people were quick to dismiss art as a silly pursuit.

Ryan loved that I was strong, and it made me want to be stronger still.

"You're welcome for bringing the band of misfits to Paris for you, Turkey."

"You're totally not getting any action tonight. You know that, right?"

He stood, taking me by the waist and walking me back to the nearest wall until I thudded softly against it. He bit his lip in that obnoxiously sexy way that made me feel powerless. "That sounds like a challenge, Turkey."

"Stop it," I laughed.

"I wonder if there are any feathers under here..." his fingertip trailed down the neckline of my dress as he pulled, popping one button free. "Oh, even better. Turkey breasts."

I swatted at him, but he caught my hand and kissed my palm. His smile faded, and his eyes grew more serious as he met my gaze. "I think I'm falling in love with you."

My went tight in my chest. "Is this part of your turkey stuffing ritual, or are you being serious?"

"I'm being serious. And no, it's not 'I think," he shook his head, eyebrows drawn together. "It is. I love you."

"I love you too, Turkey," I said.

"You can't--"

"I can't?" I asked, laughing as I walked him toward the bed and pushed him down. "Maybe you're the one who should get stuffed."

"Woah, woah, woah. I'll tell you what I told the security guard at the airport. I don't do butt stuff."

I climbed on top of him and leaned down to kiss him. He tasted so good. He always did. His hands slid across my back and then he gripped my ass and squeezed.

"Well," he said. "I'm not opposed to butt stuff if you're the one on the receiving end."

"Not happening," I said.

"Yet."

"Ever."

"We'll revisit the topic. Let's say, next week?"

"Next year."

"You drive a hard bargain, but it's a deal. I'll mark it as butt day on my calendar. We can--"

"Maybe you should stop talking and start stuffing. *Turkey*."

He flipped me over to my back and climbed on top with a grin. "You're going to enjoy regretting that."

I laughed. "That doesn't even make sense."

"It will," he said with a smirk that was absolutely loaded with promise.

PLEASE REMEMBER TO REVIEW!

Thank you so much for reading! Even if you completely hated the book (hoping you didn't!), I'm a big believer in the importance of reviews. So please don't forget to jump back on Amazon to let everyone know what you thought of the book. It's also really helpful to me, because I'm always trying to make my next book the best I've ever written, and reading feedback in my reviews is one of the best ways for me to keep working on my writing!

If the books in this series are the first you've read by me, most of my other work generally has less humor. I still slide moments in here and there, but these books have been a much-needed mental break for me where I can write about something that's not as heavy while I get over some of the frustrating things I've been dealing with in the real world.

Hope you loved it!

P.S. Stay tuned for more from this series. I've got some exciting possibilities in the works that I can't talk about quite yet, but there will be more Objects of Attraction books in the near future!

xx

Penelope

WANT BRUCE AND NATASHA'S STORY?

If you found this book before Bruce's story or William's, no worries! I tried my best to write them to be read in any order. You can find Bruce's book here (#8 bestseller on Amazon!):

H
I
S
Banana

PENELOPE BLOOM

My new boss likes rules, but there's one nobody dares to break...
No touching his banana.

Seriously. The guy is like a potassium addict.

Of course, I touched it.

If you want to get technical, I actually put it in my mouth.

I chewed it up, too... I even swallowed.

I know. Bad, bad, girl.

Then I saw him, and believe it or not, choking on a guy's banana does not make the best first impression.

I should backtrack a little here. Before I ever touched a billionaire's banana, I got my first real assignment as a business reporter. This wasn't the same old bottom-of-the-barrel assignment I always got. I wasn't going to interview a garbage man about his favorite routes or write a piece on how picking up dog poop from people's yards is the next big thing.

Nope. None of the above, thank you very much.

This was my big break. My chance to prove I wasn't a bumbling, clumsy, accident-prone walking disaster. I was infiltrating Galleon Enterprises to follow up on suspicions of corruption.

Cue the James Bond music.

I could do this. All I had to do was land the position as an intern and nail my interview with Bruce Chamberson.

Forget the fact that he looked like somebody carved him out of liquid female desire, then sprinkled on some "makes men question their sexuality" for good measure. I needed to make this work. No accidents. No disasters. No clumsiness. All I needed to do was hold it together for less than an hour.

Fast forward to the conference room before the interview, and that's where you would find me with a banana in my hand. A banana that literally had his name on it in big, black sharpie. It was a few seconds later when he walked in and caught me yellow-handed. A few seconds after that was when he hired me.

Yeah. I know. It didn't seem like a good sign to me, either.

Get His Banana (Click Here!)

WANT WILLIAM AND HAILEY'S STORY?

William and Hailey's story can be found in Her Cherry (#5 Bestseller on Amazon and Wall Street Journal Bestseller!).

How'd I meet her?
Well, a gentleman never brags.
Thankfully, I'm no gentleman.
First, I paid for her cherry (pie, but that's not the point),

Next, I deflowered her.

After that? I left my business card and walked out like I owned the place.

Yeah, you could say we hit it off.

Hailey

How did I meet William?

He walked into my bakery, bought a cherry pie, stole a vase of flowers—I still have no idea what he wanted with them—and left his business card.

Before I say what I did with the business card, I should clarify something:

William couldn't have walked into my life at a worse time.

My bakery was failing.

My creepy ex refused to leave me alone.

Oh, and I was a twenty-five-year-old virgin, a fact my friends refused to stop hassling me about.

Fixing my little virginity problem with William would be like swatting a fly with a hammer. Overkill, but the best kind.

William was stupid hot, the kind of hot that makes women do stupid things. The kind of hot that made me think *crazy* things. Like thinking the fly wouldn't even mind getting hammered by William and his washboard abs. That makes two of us.

So I called him.

Maybe it was against my better judgment. Maybe I was stepping into a disaster waiting to happen.

I knew I was in trouble when he chuckled in that deep, sexy voice of his over the phone and said, "I'm still craving your cherry. Do you deliver?"

Get Her Cherry (Click Here!)

ROMANTIC COMEDIES

LAUGH OUT LOUD
-HIS BANANA
-HER CHERRY

LIGHTER HUMOR
-SINGLE DAD NEXT DOOR
-SINGLE DAD'S VIRGIN
-SINGLE DAD'S HOSTAGE
-THE DOM'S VIRGIN
-THE BODYGUARD
-MISS MATCHMAKER

MAFIA

START HERE
HIS

-MINE
-DARK
-BABY FOR THE BEAST
-BABY FOR THE BRUTE

BDSM

START HERE
KNOCKED UP BY THE
DOM

-KNOCKED UP BY THE MASTER
-KNOCKED UP AND PUNISHED
-THE DOM'S VIRGIN
-THE DOM'S BRIDE
-PUNISHED

Don't know where to start? I hope this helps! You can also check the next page for a more detailed guide on which of my books might be best for you. Otherwise, click this image to go straight to my catalog on Amazon and start browsing.

Continue for a more detailed reading Guide ——>

I have written more or less in three distinct styles since I started two years ago. This is a more detailed breakdown of how to find which of my books might suit your interest the most:

Laugh out loud funny:

His Banana: It's not so funny that it leaves sexy and steamy by the wayside, but there are several moments that should have you laughing out loud.

Her Cherry (coming this August): Maybe even a little funnier than His Banana, at least as far as I can tell. I'm in the middle of writing this one right now, but I'm so excited to see what everyone thinks. I think it's going to be such a fun book!

Lighter Humor:

I won't go into every book here, because no one would read all that, but these books don't focus as much on silly situations. There's more emphasis on the drama of the relationship and all the usual things you've come to know and love in a romance. However, I generally think it's safe to say that you'll find comic relief in a few situations, as well as with many of the side characters in these books.

Single Dad Next Door: Mechanic gets a new neighbor, and it just so happens he needs a wife if he wants to keep his grandfather's shop. The only problem is he hates his new neighbor.

This is the book I'd recommend starting with to get a taste for my lighter romantic comedies. It has one of my all-time favorite scenes that I still smile to think about. It was also the first romantic comedy I wrote, and if you're like me, it's fun to read through an author's catalog chronologically so you can watch them grow.

Mafia:

I've done two styles of Mafia books in my career. The first series (the Citrione Crime Family) is violent, punchy, sexy, and pretty in-your-face. The men are alpha and there's kidnapping, gunfights, and all kinds of drama. If you enjoy a side of action with your romance, my debut novel, "His" is the best place to start.

If you like the mafia to be more in the background than the foreground of the story, and you don't enjoy all the violence and physical action, "Baby for the Beast" and "Baby for the Brute" are the two books for you. These spend more time focusing on the development of the relationship, but the mafia aspect still weaves itself into the story, just not in a violent sense.

BDSM:

Just like mafia, I've done a couple styles of BDSM books. One universal in my BDSM books was my goal of writing BDSM for people (like me) who are kind of put off by all the extreme elements of the kink. Everything is consensual, the Dom's are responsible (with the exception of forgetting a condom here and there for story purposes *wink*) and all the tools and toys used are light and cause no serious harm.

My most popular book across all categories by far was Knocked Up by the Dom. It's the book that ended up on the USA Today Bestseller list. If you like all the background plot to be out of the way and you want a spotlight shining right on the relationship, this is the book for you. It also comes out of the gate very very steamy and doesn't let up. The three "Knocked Up" books are probably the most smutty books in my catalog.

My BDSM books outside the Knocked Up series have a much lighter tone. The Dom's Virgin is a good place to start if you like romantic comedy and BDSM. If you feel like reading something completely different than anything you've likely read in romance, you can also check out Punished by the Prince (kind of a fantasy/BDSM/royalty/romance mashup with action and world-building).

Enemies to Lovers:

This is a category that, like the laugh out loud books, I plan to add more to this year. If you don't want the dislike between the hero and heroine to be mostly superficial, give these books a try.

They tend to be longer than my usual books and you may have to give the hero a chance before you warm up to them, but if I do my job, you'll end up loving them in the end!

Savage: Currently, this is my only published enemies to lovers book, but I'm confident it's one you'll enjoy. I also wrote a book called Hate at First Sight, but it won't be live on Amazon until around September or October. Keep an eye out for it though, I think it's a truly powerful book and maybe the best I've ever written. I can't wait to share it with everyone!

ALSO BY PENELOPE BLOOM

My Most Recent Books

His Banana (top 8 Best Seller and 3 weeks on the Amazon most sold list!)

Baby for the Beast (#60 Best Seller)

Baby for the Brute (We don't have to talk about rank on this one, do we?)

Savage (#20 Best Seller)

The Dom's Bride (#40 Best Seller)

(Babies for the Doms)

Knocked Up and Punished (top 21 Best Seller)

Knocked Up by the Master (top 12 Best Seller)

Knocked Up by the Dom (USA Today Bestselling Novel and #8 ranked Bestseller)

(The Citrione Crime Family)

His (Book 1)
Mine (Book 2)
Dark (Book 3)

Punished (top 40 Best Seller)
 Single Dad Next Door (top 12 Best Seller)
 The Dom's Virgin (top 22 Best Seller)
 Punished by the Prince (top 28 Best Seller)
 Single Dad's Virgin (top 10 Best Seller)
 Single Dad's Hostage (top 40 Best Seller)
 The Bodyguard
 Miss Matchmaker

JOIN MY MAILING LIST

Join my mailing list to make sure you never miss a new release. I generally only send an email once a month or so when I have a new book to tell you about, so don't worry about spam!

Check out my website for my sort of regular blog posts and more behind-the-scenes information about me, my books, and the author world than you'll know what to do with!

You can also find me on Facebook. I love to interact with fans, post sneak peeks for my upcoming books, host giveaways, and hear feedback!

Made in the USA
Middletown, DE
10 November 2018